THE FORTUNATE ISLES

ALSO BY LISA L. HANNETT

Bluegrass Symphony
Lament for the Afterlife
Songs for Dark Seasons
Wide Open Fear
Viking Women: Life and Lore (as Lisa Hannett)

WITH ANGELA SLATTER

Midnight and Moonshine
The Female Factory

THE FORTUNATE ISLES

STORIES

LISA L. HANNETT

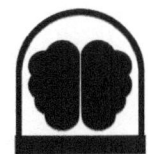

Brain Jar Press
PO Box 6687
Upper Mt Gravatt, QLD, 4122
Australia
www.BrainJarPress.com

Cover design by Peter Ball
Cover Images: *Cemetery of old ships Teriberka Murmansk* © ParStud/Depositphotos; *Beautiful Mermaid* © JEGAS_RA/Depositphotos; *Book* © tuja66/Depositphotos;

ISBN: 978-1-922479-86-0 (Ebook) | 978-1-922479-85-3 (Paperback)

For Kim
Valkyrie, sweoster, kindred spirit

Forþon him gelyfeð lyt, se þe ah lifes wyn,
gebiden in burgum, bealosiþa hwon,
wlonc on wingal, hu Ic werig oft
in brimlade bidan sceolde.

And so he little believes, he who possesses life's joy,
lives in the city, free from dangerous journeys,
proud and merry with wine, how, weary, I have often had
to survive in the sea-path.

— 'THE SEAFARER'

þæs ofereode, þisses swa mæg.

As that passed away, so this may.

— 'DEOR'

CONTENTS

INTRODUCTION

KIRSTYN MCDERMOTT

I first met Lisa Hannett, the person, in the middle of a sweltering Brisbane summer in early 2009. I was there for the Aurealis Awards and she was attending Clarion South, a gruelling live-in writers bootcamp that ran over six weeks. In Brisbane. In summer. An endurance test in more ways than one. We sat opposite each other at the post-awards breakfast, along with another Clarion South attendee, Angela Slatter – who surely needs no introduction herself these days. The two of them regaled me with stories of their time at the bootcamp thus far, and I don't think I imagined the thin edge of gleeful hysteria in their voices. They both wore colourful maxi-dresses bright enough to weary the eye of a mildly hungover Melbourne goth, and I have an equally vivid memory of Lisa explaining that they allowed themselves to procure such frocks on a weekly basis as a reward for making it through yet another seven days at Clarion South. I left Brisbane with the delightful certainty that it would not be the last I would hear of her.

I properly met Lisa Hannett, the *writer*, some two years later via her remarkable debut collection, *Bluegrass Symphony* (2011). The stories she told in that book worked together to weave a cohesive, visceral world that smelled of the prairie and fresh-cut hay, of weather-worn leathers and chickenshit scraped from the heel of a boot. A world both brutal and beautiful, inhabited by shapeshifters, vampires, minotaurs, beauty queens, and the darkest kind of carnival magic. This is what Hannett does best. She imagines worlds just one step and a briefly held breath away from our own, and conjures them with such intense and deeply tactile verisimilitude, you turn from the page expecting – if you're lucky, or if you're really not – that you might be able to travel there someday yourself.

It's what she has done again here, with *The Fortunate Isles*.

Welcome to Barradoon: a cold-climes harbour village, home to a rugged and resilient community, both close-knitted and simmering with the kind of tension that people living in each other's pockets understand all too well. Life can be hard and bellies left to hunger at times, but the sea may also be relied upon to provide a bounty – either fished, netted and harpooned, or else raided from the decks of formidably crewed longboats. Oh, and there are harpies nesting in the cliff-faces. And hippocamps and sirens and kelpies and a fickle breed of fay folk referred to only as the young strangers. You'd best stay on their good side, those strangers. And mind their rules. Wait, did I mention the mermaids? There are mermaids, and then there are *mermaids*. You'll see.

Reading this collection is a deeply immersive experience. It approaches the form of a mosaic novel, such as Hannett delivered with *Lament for the Afterlife* (2015), with several recurring characters serving as touchstones, and subsequent stories often casting new light on previously chronicled events. The opening tale, "Gutted", makes for an astonishing introduction that upends our expectations not once but twice in the first page, a warning shot across your bow. (Those mermaids, sheesh.) There is magic in the world of Barradoon as well, a ruthless sea-spun magic that threads its ambiguous, mutable way through the collection, binding the tales together. It is fickle and feral and, as Winnifletch, keeper of ravens and distiller of hex-juice, has learned: "It flies where it will" ("Ebbtide"). The same might be said for these stories. Go with them. Let their tides bear you in and out, knowing they will land you safely back on shore eventually. Probably. Possibly? For there's a salt-laced melancholy to *These Fortunate Isles*, a bittersweet tone that's equal parts delicious and traumatising. If there is a persistent refrain to the collection, it's the warning that "The Honey

Stomach" lays out, plain and simple: "In this life ... you got to give if you want to receive. No matter where that leaves you. No matter the cost." That cost can break a heart sometimes, or it can mend one. Or at least that's the hope. That's always the hope.

The writing in these stories offers a masterclass in lyricism, poetry wrought in prose, but can also be direct and unflinching when needed. Like many of the women of Barradoon, Hannett knows how to wield a filleting knife with cunning and craft. Flutes, we are told, make for unsuitable funeral music as they sound like "last breaths blown through old bones" ("A Shot of Salt Water"). The ocean is home to "thick-thighed finners with sharks' teeth in sweet lady faces and a white pointer's appetite for blood" ("Shrithing Sandwards"). The women whose lives take them to sea for ten months come home with "oar-muscled arms" and ragged pants "storm-chewed at the hems", their time away having "staved in their cheeks, chiselled the roundness from hips and breasts" and caused "blood-cracks" to split their smiles ("A Shot of Salt Water"). There are many more such lines I could lift from these pages, but I shall leave them for you to discover and delight in.

But it's the characters – the *people*, fully rounded and so well-fleshed you might continue to hear their whispers long after you've turned the final page – where this collection really shines. Winnifletch and her daughter, Shale, who desires more than anything to become a bird, preferring flight and feathers to sails and ships. The tanglesmith, Bøda, who learns that magic knitted from an angry, wounded heart is the hardest to unpick, to make good – even if that was what she wanted. The young lad, Fallon, risking life and limb on a cliff-climb in pursuit of a harpie-bride, realising the love he truly longs for is grounded in the earth below. And Rowe, dear Rowe, stumbled upon as a squalling babe in a rockpool by her adoptive father. Rowe, who had never fitted in – not with her family, not in the village of Barradoon, not with anything – until finally she does. Her journey stretches between two stories and culminates in "Ebbtide", the tale that closes the collection. It's a pitch-perfect ending, fiercely triumphant yet resisting an easy resolution, as do so many of its companion tales. Perhaps this is what makes *The Fortunate Isles* such an engaging, intriguing and unforgettable book. There are no neatly tied bows here and plenty of loose threads at which to keep picking. Hannett is a writer who trusts her readers to listen and look closely, to be open to wonder and terror both, and to understand the cost.

So, come. Drink a shot of salt water for luck, or for grief, and sink yourself into the chill waters of Barradoon. You will be well rewarded, even if you leave with a few extra scars.

Kirstyn McDermott
February 2023
Ballarat, Australia

GUTTED

Erl doesn't believe in selkies.

The only skins women in his village discard are covered in scales, separated from juicy white flesh at the points of their gutting knives. Twice a day, fisherwives make short work of the fleet's catch. Dawn and dusk see them straddling mermaids' torsos, cleaning plump tails with efficient, intuitive slices. Thigh-length fillets slap into piles on the jetty while bloodless heads, grey shoulders and breasts splash back into the ocean. Waters churn as surviving merfolk wrestle to feed on the scraps.

Around here, seals are a rare sight.

He's watched local women work countless times: always removing skins, tossing them seaward, never donning them. Even so, for six nights running he's set out with Filcher's crew, armed with gobbets of red meat (not yet turned rancid) to placate the region's mermaids. To distract them while a ship's worth of men hunt for Odessa, his absentee wife.

I feel trapped, she'd told him a week ago.

'Just you wait, Erl. We'll find that selkie bitch.'

Erl's bearded jaw clenches every time Filcher speaks. No skipper should care so much about his first mate's missus. Filcher's expression is haunted: the lines in his face, weathered as canyons, are depthless in the moonlight. His palms are rubbed raw from handling salt-crusted nets, as are the rest of the crew's. Erl's scarred knuckles whiten, his broad fingers crack into fists.

I just need some space, Odessa had said.

You can't leave, he'd replied. Quietly, to avoid waking the children.

'Two black bobbers,' the captain barks. 'Off the starboard bow.'

Erl grunts, ignores the note of hope in Filcher's voice. Odds are the fisherman's spotlight will sweep across a pair of buoys or a brace of seagull corpses—sure as hell won't be a couple of selkies. He leans against the larboard rail and waits for the string of curses that will confirm his doubts. No, Erl doesn't believe in women zipping themselves into magic seal skins, swimming off, never to return. However Filcher, still duped by fickle love, does.

As do Erl's children.

The captain's wild story, Erl had thought, was the perfect explanation. The truth was too painful. So he'd lined his kids up first thing in the morning, five boys and one girl, on the wooden blanket box that sat at the foot of his empty bed. The eldest lifted the youngest onto his lap—their high cheekbones and dark hair were so like Odessa's it hurt Erl to see them—then twelve bleary eyes focused.

You're stifling me, she'd said.

In all his life, he'd never spun such an important tale. What was it Filcher had told him? What had the skipper said his girl had done? Erl had to get the details straight.

Breathing deeply, he inhaled the present and expelled the past. The room smelled of pine and lemon, detergent and salty air; comforting, scrubbed-clean scents he'd prayed would bleach the previous night from his memory. The kids didn't notice his jitters.

Instead, their eyes had grown wide, then wider, as he settled into his story. They'd all heard of selkies—even Pearl, who'd only started school that year—but they'd had no idea their Ma was one of them. Warming to his lie, Erl told them how bewitching Odessa had been at seventeen; how she'd always been tempted by shore men like him; how she'd shed her ravaged sealskin and promised any repayment for saving her from the mermaids.

One thing only would make him happy, he'd decided then, and that was to keep her. All to himself.

There's someone else, she'd said.

They'd married before the week's end. He'd taken her home, locked her pelt away in the very box upon which the children now sat. It was for her own good: he would keep it safe to keep her from further temptation.

A fisherman's life wasn't exciting but Odessa had seemed content. Erl did his duty, filled her belly with child after child. She'd been too busy to grow bored, or so he'd thought. But as her shore children grew her thoughts turned to the infants she'd left behind in the sea. No doubt they'd wound up victims to merfolk, if they'd somehow survived all these years alone. Her imagination strayed, as it had the day she'd met Erl, taking her to unexplored realms. Her mind wandered—her body followed soon after.

It's over. Let me go.

She had sworn she didn't love the six bairns on land any less than the six in the deeps; but it was the latter's turn for attention, for her time and protection. Nothing could change her mind. Nothing did. And so she'd left.

'Forever?' the kids had asked.

'Yes, forever.'

'Can we have her skin? The magic one with the flippers and whiskers and tail? We could put it on; we could find her.'

'She took it with her, didn't she?' he'd said, his voice wavering, gaze dropping to the blanket box. 'The minute I turned my back, we were betrayed.'

Let me go, Erl.

'You should've held her tighter, Da. You should've made her stay.'

'I tried. Honest.'

'But what are we going to do now?'

Let me go—

'Forget her.'

The kids wailed. Their grief reached a decibel that could shatter ice—it echoed across the bay, caught Filcher's ear, dragged him around to Erl's cabin.

'Odessa?' the captain had called, throwing the familiar door wide. 'Love, what's wrong? What's—'

Erl had looked at his friend, at his skipper, their faces mirrors of bewilderment. Filcher's head whipped from side to side; his chest heaved from exertion, but also distress. No one would run so quickly, barge into another man's house so easily, unless he'd had good reason.

Understanding crept across Erl's features, weighing him down, leaving him listless. 'Save your breath, mate. She's gone.'

'Mamma's a sea monster,' Pearl cried, tears gobbing down her face. 'She's took her skin and skipped out on us, back to them watery kids.'

For a moment, Filcher's expression matched that of the girl's; then his flushed face had purpled with anger.

'Goddamn selkies!'

The kids flinched in unison and fell silent. Erl had remained still, his fury already spent. Nothing could be done about Filcher's trespass, not now.

I can't breathe, she'd said.

'Fuck that, Erl. We're getting her back, soon as dark hits.'

Erl, I can't breathe.

He'd nodded, despite his exhaustion. 'You'd best prepare for a long night then, *mate.*'

'Caught anything for us?' The fisherwives' blades glint peach and rose in the sunrise, their cutting edges smeared with raw innards.

'Nope,' Erl says. 'Skipper's got us fishing for a ghost.'

The women click their tongues, shake their heads knowingly. 'Them ghosts is more trouble than merfolk, but don't yield nowhere near as much meat.'

'They say phantom flesh lasts for eight days,' Erl replies. 'Two more nights of this shit and I'm done.'

Two more nights, he thinks, feet dragging. His boots crunch up the shale path home, an exhausted sound like grinding bones. His heart races as he approaches the front door—but when he enters, the house is quiet as a secret. The children don't stir as he wakes the sitter, sends her away with a pocketful of coins. Performing a ritual that's taken less than a week to become habit, Erl closes and locks his bedroom door, opens both windows to let in the fresh morning air. He undresses and folds his clothes, crouches naked in front of the blanket box, and turns the key.

Inside, his hand brushes the softest skin he's ever touched, even fairer now for lack of blood. Salting has kept the smell down, but has stiffened the meat. He sweeps long chestnut curls to one side of the plastic-lined compartment, a tender but functional caress. Moving quickly, he hacks away chunks of stomach and hip for tomorrow's bait. Two more nights and the evidence will be gone, leaving only the shell of his heartbreak. Arms that had lost their embrace long before they were stilled, legs without promise of happiness. An empty, beautiful, soulless face.

Let me go.

He shuts the box's lid and climbs into bed. In his dreams, hinges whine and fingernails scrape against wood. A muffled voice echoes, begging forgiveness. Over and over, scratching and creaking and mumbling, until waves pound it all to silence.

A RIGHT PRETTY MATE

Fallon's palms weren't yet callused. His fingers were sea-softened, and he fancied they were gently webbed; better shaped for paddling than climbing. Each nail was blunt as a seal's nose, not sharp like Mither's, despite her relentless nipping and filing and grooming, her daily tugging at his little digits, at his disappointing limbs. Wings flapping, she yanked one arm, then the other, while he clung to the foot of their feather bed, or the porch rail, or the stool by the cottage hearth. She *pulled* while he resisted—not the idea of growth, mind, but the ache in his joints as she tried to stretch him, the clear futility of it all.

Didn't work yesterday, Fallon thought, rubbing his elbows between bouts. *Won't work today neither.*

Folk 'round here weren't known to give up easy.

No matter if they were lady-faced birds—as proud of their pinions and pterodactyl feet as they were of their lustrous tresses and perfect noses—and no matter if they were the hairy-chested and fully-fleshed men who mated with them, they all fought to raise their families well above the waterline. To lift them higher and higher. To revel in the flattering sun-gold, the sky's open-armed promise.

But Fallon was too little for such lofty stuff. Too shy to strut for the lasses, to preen. Though Mither reminded him, most days, of the pains she endured to have him, Fallon sometimes wondered if he was more cuckoo than harpy-born runt. He simply wasn't built like other lads in his brood; he had none of their physical gifts. The tanned and striated muscles. The effortless extension and head for heights. The impossible, sinewed reach.

Both his hands together would barely cup one harpy egg, he thought, even if he was careful. Fallon was always careful.

That spring at least a dozen bolder boys turned thirteen with Fallon. A set of hard-eyed squidders come up the coast from Gallahorn way. The puffineer's son from down south. Local triplets destined for the whalery, what with those broad shoulders, that fisherman's gait. A pair of thick-tongued mouth-breathers whose sires bred too close to the clutch. Nearer home, Fallon's two freckled cousins came of age. Plus his best pal Ril, who'd split from his mam's nethers a week after the rest, so had to wait that much longer for his chance to go a-gathering on Lundey island. To scale those pocked fowling cliffs and choose the best nest, the right harpy egg. To find his first and only mate.

Of course, *Ril* had nothing to worry about. Seven days shy of his birthday, he was already a curly head taller than any of the other would-be's and well-wishers on shore; forced to hunker as proud harpies swooped overhead, singing good luck to the boys wading to rowboats moored in the shallows. Ril's jaw was strong from a lifetime of casual defiance, cheeks and arms pink-striped with ragged scars; fair price, Fallon thought, for frequently pissing off his fast-clawed mam. Tormenting his sleeping sisters by plucking their tail feathers; gobbling their smoked cod when they were pre-ovulating and hungriest. Teasing his dam, saying he might not even bother egg-hunting at all. Saying, *Now how does that tide turn ya, Ma?* Saying, *Plenty chuffed with Fal's company, thanks all the same.* Saying, *How many more chicks do we need 'round here anyway?*

Saying things Fallon would never dare.

Ril's mam forgave him again and again.

Down at the wharves, whenever the old dogs'd let him, Ril turned lathes at their shipyard. He scraped barnacles off hulls easy as knifing lard. He mucked out bilges, clambered from deck to crow's-nest in seconds, lithe on the rigging. He worked the sweeps like nobody's business, but claimed he rowed furthest with good ol' Fal as cox.

'Cos I'm so friggin light, Fallon thought. Flushing, he bobbed in a dory twenty feet offshore, wishing they'd let him swim out to the Lundey instead. He was much more graceful under water than on it. The heavy sea held him down, compressed him, made him substantial. He didn't need gaping-wide skies: in cold-rushing currents, Fallon *flew*.

Submerged, his body soared. It wasn't some half-formed, featherless thing. It didn't rely on Mither or Ril. It wasn't afraid of falling.

Given the chance, Fallon would fin across the channel, quick as a carp, and reach the island before the other lads had even locked oars. He'd un-nest an egg with a bright abalone shimmer, race it home, and be paired.

Fool boy, the birds tutted when he'd suggested it, flicking their hair, ruffling crests. *Right from the word go, you got to care for your lady—her shell's too delicate for all that splashing. You got to* sail *your girl landwards, keep her safe and warm and dry. Or, what? You keen to wind up alone?*

Guppies squirmed in his bowels when the first foghorn sounded. Thirteen minutes 'til the horn called the boys back in again. Thirteen minutes to get themselves wed.

Instantly, oars plunked into the water—with a whoop, young gatherers heaved. All but Fallon, who was really too small to steer his boat solo; the paddles turned awkwardly in his grip, promising blisters more than propulsion. He paused, closed his eyes, exhaled. Focused on the mid-morning sun, hot on his raw neck. The comforting scent of salt and bait and tarred clinkers. The lulling waves.

He pictured Ril on the crossbench before him. The languid rhythm of his stroke. The curve of his shoulders and spine. No matter what Mither said, this posture wasn't an affected, lazy slump, but a sign of trust. With Fallon, Ril let down his guard.

Deep breaths as he tried to muster some of the other boy's ease, his pluck.

'Go'on, Fal,' the real Ril hollered from the beach. 'I'll be catching you up soon enough, you don't get your arse moving!'

Fallon cracked a lid, spied Ril laughing, flicking a long strand of kelp like a whip. A few days and Ril would have his go; he'd get the best mate of all...

For a second, Fallon was tempted to shout back, *Come on then, ya loon! Hop in!* But with Mither's caw resounding overhead, he clamped lips and hands, leaned back on the plank the way Ril had taught, feet planted wide, and sculled.

The chicks looked different, depending on where their nests were tucked on the island, how high their caverns. The most gorgeous lasses were laid nearly two hundred metres skywards, right below the Lundey's meadowed plateau. Most harpies hadn't the wing-power to haul their heavy bellies to such heights, not with the laying-pangs on them. Those that could came from strong stock. The parcels left up there were off-white, freckled—definite two-handers—just like the babes they eventually bore. Topside girls' hair was thick and sun-bleached, their down soft on full-figured bodies.

Last year, Fallon watched his eldest sister fail to elevate her unborn girl. Poor Trix had huffed her swollen gut across the channel, claws clipping the surface, tawny wings scraping a headwind, sights fixed on the island's distant, uppermost tier... But with a fat egg so close to dropping, she'd had to settle on a shit-spattered nook 'round about the hundred-metre mark, a hole no gatherer had yet seen fit to plunder. Now, Fallon had no intention of wedding his sister's kid—no kin-kisser, him—but he'd aimed to soothe, saying *Give it time, Trix,* saying, *Plenty of babes come from those central nests,* thinking: *Ril's mam, for one.* Opal-eyed, loam-skinned, with a fine display of fox-fire plumage—half the men in town cursed their luck sorely after missing out on collecting *her*.

As he rowed, a feral breeze caught the spray, lashed it against Fallon's back. Droplets slid off the oilskin sling knotted over his shoulder, but soon his singlet was saturated. Seawater coursed along the arse of his snug shorts, 'til it seemed he'd pissed himself. Lungs and arms pumping, he drew on the oars, the soak cool against flushed skin, bare thighs and neck already crisping with burn. Far behind, keels thunked against stone as the quickest lads reached the island. He didn't need to turn to know they were now over the gunwales, now ascending the rock face, now easily swinging from one dark recess to the next. Keeping pace with Fallon's boat, Mither narrated the rise of this boy and that, making it sound like each was more squirrel than man, each more man than him.

'Kit Gallahorn's past the algae,' she cawed, spitting a gob against the curse of snagging a slime-born. Easiest to reach, the lowest fruit was most often worm-ridden—all gatherers knew that for truth. *Get above the scum-line*, every sire agreed, *before burrowing in. Go for the first hole, you'll mate yerself to a rank old bird, believe you me: a boneless chick, or one with fin-danglers, with a tongue like milk-skin, or with her inner bits slipped outer...*

'Faster, kid! Look: Berton's already swung above the crumble!' Mither gouged her talons into Fallon's prow, and hauled.

You get but one chance, the dads had said. *Aim high, lads, else you'll scoop yerself a rotter.*

'It's just you and the dimwits now, son. And only six minutes to blow! Hurry!'

A jolt as Fallon's skiff collided with rock. Until late afternoon, the island's shore-side would be sunlit from water to skyline; the boy squinted against its ochre glare, craned his head, shaded his eyes with a shaking hand. Impossible to see the peak from here, but he could imagine its nauseating height. There were no ropes to safeguard the collectors, no zigzagging paths to guide them on the slick limestone; they'd make it up on their own, or not at all. Lads were fast-moving, muscles limned with morning gold; if there were any grunts of exertion, any whimpers, Fallon couldn't hear them. Any prayers were pecked dumb by a hundred thousand beaked critics. Puffins and guillemots gossiped in crevices, wheeling and watching, cackling at the gangly creatures scrambling for love.

Harpies batted smaller birds away, clearing handholds for their sons. Feathered matriarchs cheered the climbers on. One, closest to Fallon's ear, squawking: 'Five minutes, boy. *Move!*'

Time wobbled, bad as his legs. Air squeaked in and out. No feeling in his face, or his wet-ribbon limbs. *I can't do this.* Time rocked like the bench underfoot, shaking him loose. Movements jerked from minute to minute, strobed beneath a flock of thundering wings. *I can't do this—* The boat fell away, the cliff jammed into palms and knees and feet. 'Four and a half!' *I can't—* Vision reduced to a fist-sized blur, skimming over algae and weed-cluttered holes and oyster-blobs that once were eggs. 'That's it, kid! Go!' Time juddered. Now he was beyond the reek of those rejects. *I can't—* and he was past the chalk line, Mither shouting, 'Three!' and 'Left! Left!' and he overshot the point of Trix's letdown, 'Keep going! Veer right!' and *Maybe* the nests were beckoning, larger, neater at this level, 'Don't settle, child! You still got two minutes!' and *Maybe I can* 'Go go go!' and zephyrs whistled across dry hollows, primal music promising forever, carrying sweet scents of sunbaked leaves.

I'm going to make it, he thought. Not to the top, not even close, but high enough. A thrill sizzled through him, bloomed in his guts, and for one magic second he believed it.

Jamming his toes into a vertical crease, Fallon braced as best he could. Two likely nests gaped, a full stretch above him. Gravel skittered as he adjusted position, as he quaked, cursed his stubby limbs, inched upwards.

'Choose,' Mither called, the shrill gone from her voice, tones pitched to finish this deal. 'Just under a minute, cockerel. There's a fine blue-black at two o'clock, a dappled fancy at eleven. Good shape on both, a good sheen. Either'd make you a right pretty mate, kid. All's you gotta do is claim her.'

Steeling himself, Fallon reached up to the left, *willing* his arms longer, *straining*, fingers waggling for the nest's open mouth. His nails grazed the cavern's lip—*so close!*—and he went for a second swipe. Fallon pitched to the side, overcorrected. Too far—*too far!*—'Too far!'

Time, and the boy, slipped.

There's a damned murk on the water, Fallon thought, lying on his back in a cramped canoe, rocking, rocking. *The chop's way too rough for catching fish.*

He fumbled for some tackle—or tried to. There was a lid on this boat; he couldn't sit up, couldn't turn his head. The craft's narrow sides crushed his arms, squeezed them tight. *Won't catch nothing this way*, he thought, panic rising. No reel, no wriggle room, no sun to bait a lure by. Why'd he come out after dark? *This is all wrong.* Humidity walloped him, right in the face, hot and damp as breath, yet he shivered 'til his teeth rattled. *Where's Ril?* Fallon never set out fishing without him. Side to side, side to side, he swayed, cramped and cold and *wrong*. He was drenched; the storm tossing his vessel added drop after drop to the wet.

Where is *it?* he thought, grasping for that hard thing he'd lost.

'Where's my rod?'

'Here now,' Ril whispered, hugging Fallon close, rocking, rocking. 'I gotcha.'

Brine stung Fallon's eyes as he opened them, sun-sparks catching in his lashes. The throbbing in his temples wasn't helped by Ril's persistent to-and-froing, or the volume of his joyous, 'S'alright, Henny-Bea! Fal's come good!'

A cyclone of wings as Mither landed on the shale beside them. Younger chicks flocked to Ril's shout, responding to his tear-stained relief. *The birds love him*, Fallon thought, though Ril paid them little mind. Girls cooed and gabbled for his attention, 'til it was clear his focus belonged to the boy in his lap. Snubbed, the fledgling harpies flapped back to their mates, pretending their partners, their *men*, were finer, fitter specimens than Ril.

Smiling down at Fallon, he sucker-punched him in the ribs. 'You off your nut? What's with the daredevil act?'

'What?' Wheezing, Fallon propped himself against Ril's thighs, took a look at himself. Pebble-studded gashes shorn into his calves, a chunk torn from one knee, forearms and palms streaked red. His pulse thumped in grazes on his cheeks and chin. His thin shirt was smeared with grit and blood, its straps shredded where Mither had scrabbled to catch him.

'I fell.'

He'd overbalanced, or the foothold had given out, and the speed of the plummet had been deafening, pain had scraped him from toe to tip, and gulls and gannets had shrieked with the guillemots as he dropped, but Mither was louder than all them. Fifteen beats, tops, harpy spurs seizing, puncturing his shoulders... Slowing him—right?—slowing him for ten or ten thousand seconds—right?—slowing him before the foghorn summoned the lads home—slowing him enough to slam onto a slippery shelf, to make a desperate grab through puke-coloured ooze, to latch onto something solid and oval...

'I got one.' Fallon watched the new husbands overturning their boats on shore, large eggs strapped safely across puffed chests. Mams crowing about their sons, dads cuffing flushed ears, then adjusting the lads' slings, correcting their nursing techniques; by three days at the outside they'd be mating. Stomach sinking, Fallon said, 'Didn't I?'

'Don't worry about that,' Ril began, but Fallon shoved him. He *had*, hadn't he? Trembling onto all fours, he waved off Mither's attempts to right him. He scowled as if thoughts and brows would mutually come together. Before his chin had smashed against the ledge, knocking him dizzy, before Mither'd wrenched him away from the wall, before the horn'd bellowed, before he'd plunged into the cold blue, Fallon *had* done it. A low grab, sure, but he *had* collected...

'Where is she?'

'Fal,' Ril said, and there was such sadness in that one syllable, Fallon knew he'd made a mistake.

How many more chicks do we need 'round here anyway?

Given time, he could've been happy on his own. Better that than being saddled with a monster. Better that than choosing the wrong mate.

'Leave the man be,' Mither said, nudging Ril aside.

There was an unfamiliar shuffle in her gait, leathered legs snug beneath her flanks, speckled abdomen dragging. In thirteen years, Fallon hadn't seen his mam alight for more than a flutter of seconds, much less *walk*. That waddle was meant as a kindness, he realised. Mither was hiding his shame in that undercarriage of hers. She was protecting him.

'Let me see her,' he said, blushing at the unmanly break in his voice. He coughed, tried again. 'Now, Mither.'

'Don't got to ask me twice,' she said, though he *had*, and she smiled because of it, and she winked, and she stood.

The egg was plain: pure white with a glow of bone-china blue. Unremarkable, solid, smooth. A blessing given its origin. It could've been jaundiced or congealed. It could've been crawling with sea lice. It could've been *off*.

Didn't seem to be, though. As he and Ril tramped along the beach, piling driftwood and dried weed in a wheelbarrow, Fallon snuck a whiff of the ovule swaddled under his thickest sweater. A mild goat-cheese pong, a trace of sulphur, but not bad. Not too bad.

'Let's go back,' Ril said, tossing gnarled silver branches onto the teetering stack. Pebbles clacked as the lads steered and stopped, a sound like an abacus tallying. Their haul *would* be toted; timber for burning was scarce and any lumber worth its grain was shaped into clinkers, masts, oars. Lots were drawn, shifts allocated, boys paired to scour the drift at low tide. Ril had fixed to partner with Fallon, bless him. Right about now, Fal couldn't have stomached anyone else's company.

'C'mon, man. I'm freezing my sack off out here. Let's go back.'

'Not yet,' Fallon said, hefting the load at his breast. Licking the boys' feet, the chill pre-dawn tide soughed in. Wind yawned across drowsy waves. 'Give me a sec.'

Ril adjusted his grip on the barrow. Poised to push, his lips pursed, he waited. A lantern swung from one polished handle, casting weird shadows. In the near darkness, twigs danced like sea-grass in a winter current. Arms aching, Fallon watched them writhe.

What he wouldn't give to put his pointless egg down for a while. To splash out into the sea, and dive.

Three days had been and gone.

Yesterday, the whaler-triplets took their turn out to the Lundey and back. By late afternoon, their mates had hatched: full-plumed, thick-boned creatures who'd doubled in size by moonrise. From the looks, these new harpies were bound to be large as walruses. 'They'd want to be big,' Ril had said at the girls' welcoming feast. 'What with them huge bastards fixed to mount 'em.' Due to climb last, Ril observed the night's proceedings closely. 'Bet they're hoping for daughters. Any sons'll wreck 'em as breeders for certain.'

Fallon knew he'd have to squat with his chick too, soon as—*if*—she appeared. Husbands got familiar with their hens straight from the shell, always had. Roosting brought lads right close to their mates, immediately, intimately, or so Mither said. It got them used to being on top.

For three days Fallon had lugged his egg around, pressed it against his belly, nestled with it in bed. Three days with Mither hovering, nagging. *Hold her upright. Knot that sling tighter else she'll fall out. A bit of crooning won't go astray, kid.* Three days of rocking and plumping pillows and cooing himself hoarse, and still Fallon's bird hadn't shifted.

And still Fallon felt nothing when he held it.

The thing was a stone. No sign, not a grey whisker of cracking on the white. With each hour, Fallon was sure it got heavier. 'She's filling out for ya,' Ril had said, sketching busty curves in the air. Fallon had forced a laugh, but thought, *Or maybe she's got the death-bloats. Maybe she's turning to muck, filling with gas. Maybe she's going to explode like Paltry Orr's did that time...*

And if so?

If he was warming a bucket of sludge and soft bones?

If his lass was anything but? If she was some half-formed beast, clear as a jellyfish, just as gutless? If she hadn't the brawn, the salt, to be a mam?

If she was a useless runt like him?

Well, he'd deal with it, wouldn't he, like Mither had instructed. He'd smash the spoiled thing, churn its contents to chum. Give the rancid slop to crabbers, or treat the gulls. Once the last speck was gobbled, he'd steal back home while the harpies were out; he'd tie extra trousers, long-johns and slicker in his quilt, grab rod and reel, flint and steel, and leave.

No goodbyes, Fallon knew, for the likes of him.

East or west, he'd follow the coast until the Lundey was well out of sight. Until he'd gone far enough not to be a burden.

After feeding the bonfire, Fallon crouched, parching-close. On the bay's dark waters, lightly salted with constellations, two local lads got an early start on their gathering day. Not an hour past, the final Gallahorn harpy had pecked into the world. Just now, the hook-nosed puffineer's had unfurled her gorgeous black limbs. Celebrations were kicking up from wharves to dunes, rum dousing the clutch's newest members. Across the way, the rapid slap and crack of paddles on the ocean echoed with enthusiasm. A rhythm of continued success.

While dawn spilled its own yolk over the horizon, Fallon's seamless egg still slept.

'Tell you what,' Ril said, lobbing periwinkles onto the coals. 'That bulb of yours proves to be a dud, I'll snatch a spare for ya. Just keep the thing whole for a few more days, and we'll be sweet.'

Fallon snorted. 'Think yer that good, do ya? Last I checked, you only had two arms. How you supposed to carry all that? Planning on tiptoeing down the Lundey? Free-falling into yer dory?'

'Hmmm.' Ril's expression turned serious. Whoops sailed joyous across the water. Paddles slapped, cracked. 'How 'bout this, then? You can have mine if you want.'

Flames guttered between them. Legs splayed, Ril sat on an upturned pail, his not-lazy slouch relaxed as ever. As if the offer was no big deal. As if it hadn't wound Fallon's stomach into a tizzy.

As if he could even contemplate a future that had no Ril in it.

His gob flapped for a response.

Paddles slapped, cracked.

'And what're you gonna do without—'

'What'm I gonna do *with* one, Fal?' The question yanked Ril's voice an octave higher. He half-stood, expression part panic, part defeat. The fire cracked, louder and louder. Paddles slapped and *cracked*... 'Don't ya think— I mean, couldn't you and me just be—'

A hard thudding struck Fallon's ribcage, the likes of which he'd never felt before. A deep shudder winded him, set him adrift. A second later, his belly was slick, lukewarm goo dripping down his thighs.

'Ril,' he whispered, hardly believing it. 'What'm I supposed to do?'

'Give her some air,' Mither shrieked, swooping, it seemed, out of nowhere. Fallon jumped. Albumen slopped out of the sling as he fumbled at the knot behind his neck, while talons snagged and shredded his sweater. 'I got this,' he croaked, batting her off. 'I got this, Ma!'

Or so he hoped.

The hen wriggled much more than expected. With a final resounding crack, the shell splintered. Shards sloughed away, slicing Fallon's belly, and he leapt up at the pain, then thought twice—what if he dropped her?—so flopped back to the ground, bracing and cradling simultaneously, making a mess of both. 'What do I do now,' he squeaked, tangled in his sleeves, fabric pulsing against his torso as sodden wings bashed for dear life.

'Get her out,' shouted Mither, as if Fallon wasn't *trying*. Ducking through his collar, he struggled to get loose of sweater and swaddling. What a stink! Iron and onion and sour milk. A monstrous—a monster's —stench. Fallon swallowed bile and tears. A healthy lass couldn't gouge him this way, with nails puncturing left and right sides at once. A proper-shaped harpy only had one mouth; she couldn't suckle at his navel while also mewling for seed. She couldn't bounce on his lap while also clawing around to his back. She shouldn't have four wings.

'Oh, Fallon,' Mither breathed as the beast finally splatted onto the shale, half in front of him, half behind.

Burying his face in the crook of his elbow, Fallon wept. 'I'm sorry,' he said, barely audible above the creature's frightful chattering. 'I'm sorry.'

'Quit yer bawling, love,' Mither said, now giggling, now crying along with him. 'Save yer energy for these beauties. You're gonna need it!'

Bleary-headed, Fallon saw the bonfire flailing. The sky above dappled with harpies coming in for a gander. The nest-spotted island looming in the distance. The shore swarming with uncles and untested boys, all wielding full bottles, all red-cheeked with pride. The pebbles at his feet shining with gore.

Both in front and behind him, a sweet dove of a lass.

Grey-flocked, green-eyed, vixen-haired. Skin the hue of twilight, teats round as the moon. Identical lips stretched wide with hunger, revealing pointed teeth. Four wings, all told: a perfect pair for each twin.

'What do you say, Ril,' Fallon said, as Mither strutted and crowed. 'Wanna go halves?'

No crude answer. No full-knuckled punch of approval. At some point between the break and the drop, Ril had gone.

What luck the twins meant for Fallon's brood! What good fortune for the whole clutch! Twice the beauty, twice the joy. Twice the chance for more sons.

Twice the nerves.

One bird would've been more than enough—but this? How was he supposed to squat on both of them? At the same time? Separately? What if he couldn't? What if they wouldn't?

This bothered Fallon as much as anything; two nights had passed and the hens'd shown him not a flick of interest. Even after their nethers had *bloomed*. Even after Mither'd shoved the three of them into the nursery together. Even after she'd brought whiskey-soaked seed for the girls, cups of black screech for him. Even after they'd gorged themselves, made themselves giddy. Even after he'd sung that stupid courting tune.

The lasses groomed each other's plumage, filed each other's talons. They lapped each other's hair clean, pinched the fleas from each other's scalps. They plucked down from each other's hides, stuffed a small mattress. In a secret language, they wished each other goodnight and dozed under each other's wings. They shared no kisses with him.

Fallon's girls were an instant, exclusive clique of two.

He reckoned it *must* be different for men with only one mate. A single hen would look first to her husband, wouldn't she? He'd introduce her to life, and laughter, and eventually love. He'd be her perch, and she his roost. Isn't that how these things went?

Ril would know, but Fallon couldn't ask. What with his own gathering due, Ril had other stuff on his mind. That's why he hadn't come 'round the cottage these past few days. That's why he scarpered when Fallon brought the twins to the beach. That's why he was too damned busy to push a barrow with his best friend.

That had to be why.

Two shots of bourbon, a mug of spiced rum, and Fallon was good and sloshed.

Season ended with Ril's outing tomorrow, so folk were bent on cramming a year's worth of carousing into this one night. Hurricane lamps topped whiskey barrels on the strand, the innards of both adding a ruddy glow to revellers' faces. Kelp garlands strung on poles corralled drinkers and dancers. Scrubbed tarps on the banks offered clean places to take a load off, or pass out. Ale jugs glinted in the firelight. The bottoms of glass after glass reflected the stars. Fiddlers sawed through the crowd while harpies chirped airborne choruses. Some birds ruffled dune grasses with their mates, but not Fallon's girls, no sirree. Mither was showing them off to any and everyone, chuffed as though she'd laid them herself.

Unsteady on his feet though he was, Fallon had no trouble sneaking away.

Ankle-deep in the shallows, he cocked his head and sized up the Lundey. *Reckon I could do it in ten.* He could do that much, even if he couldn't be a true husband. He downed a half-pint, spat the dregs. Nary a gust, the channel's surface like silk— *Yeah,* he thought. *Ten minutes, easy done.* Swerving, he caught another eyeful of the hoopla up the beach. What with the suds passing around, the drums getting folk frenzied, the hens whistling and winking and flashing their tits... What with him being invisible... Who'd care if he climbed that fucking island faster than any other man?

He'd know.

He'd care.

And if Ril ever talked to him again, he'd believe it.

Fallon shucked trousers and shirt; the first belt of cold shrivelled his balls, cleared some of the fumes from his head. He swam underwater, silent as a ripple, 'til his lungs burned. Legs powering him forward, short arms sweeping gallons aside. He gave in to instinct, followed the retreating tide. Soon he outswam the racket on shore. In its place, an ancient hush bubbled from beneath, peaceful, reassuring. Pulsing with the thrum of solitude.

Each stroke marked seconds, minutes. He reached the Lundey's algaed foot in half the time it'd taken to row there. Confident, he submerged again. Darting 'round to the seaward cliff, he got his bearings, uttered a prayer, and began to climb.

There was no foghorn urging him on, no timekeeper noting his progress, no Mither screeching orders—but Fallon *knew* he was fast. The moon silvered every handhold, every nook. None were beyond reach, none taunted or eluded him. He soared past the sludge layer, the limestone, the chalk. Seven minutes, max, and barely a third to go. Higher, faster. Gasping for breath. He spied dozens—*hundreds!*—of unclaimed gals, just sitting in the shadows, waiting for a touch. *Keep moving.* Startled guillemots snapped at him, protective mams threatening to spear. Eight minutes, maybe nine, and *there*. Hear that? Was that the trill of larks? The rustle of wind through a fine lawn. He couldn't stop to listen carefully, not now, not so close. And *there*. Smell that? Buttercups and corncockles and candytufts; the sweet perfume of a secluded meadow. *Keep moving.*

He reached up, fingers closing on soft blades of grass.

I did it, he thought, then said it aloud, as if truth needed volume. 'I did it.'

It made no difference to Fallon that he couldn't hoist himself onto the sward. The angle was too precarious; there was nothing long enough up there for him to seize, nothing below to give him a solid boost. He'd made it to the apex. Higher and faster than any other lad, regardless of flexibility or muscle tone. *He'd* made it.

Savouring the moment, Fallon lowered his knees onto the ledge of a glorious, top-shelf eyrie. He gripped the gently arched entrance and, shaking with excitement, eased himself down and in.

'Us two might've been mates,' he whispered, shifting to avoid crushing a small, wind-hardened egg. No matter, no matter. He'd had his chance, he'd picked his nest—let the twins go and lie in it. He patted his pocket for a bottle, then recalled he'd left his pants on land. *Besides*, he thought, hearing Ril's deep voice, *How many more chicks do we need 'round here anyway?*

Fallon woke with his skull pounding, a stone under his jaw, another lodged behind his sternum.

In the distance, a foghorn moaned.

What a drunken fool he'd been, scaling the Lundey with a bellyful, telling no one his plans... How Ril'd cackle to find Fallon trapped here. 'Gone and pulled the possum-in-a-chimney routine, haven't ye,' he'd say, not even trying to keep a straight face. 'Racing up, up, up, not sparing a thought for how to get back down again.'

If only Ril was here.

After peeling the crust from his lashes, Fallon worked his lids open. Even this tiny movement made his innards heave. Too slow, he spewed mid-roll, then lay there blinking beside the thin yellow puddle, cheek mashed against damp stone. As weak now as he'd been last night, after the thrill of the climb had ebbed along with his gumption. Clouds had scudded across the moon—and not that she gave off any heat, but everything had seemed so much colder without her light. Soon Fallon's teeth chattered. His feelers numbed stiff. *Ten minutes up*, he'd thought, creeping to the edge, peering over. *Ten seconds down...*

Guppy-limbed at the prospect, he'd wedged himself into the nest's deepest corner, egg or no egg. Now the sun was two large hands above the horizon and the cavern was stifling. Small wonder the lass he'd supplanted had been baked harder than Mither's bread. Up here, the air was hot and ripe and thick with starbursts that sparked to the beat of his hangover.

He lay back. Salt-water pooled in his collarbone hollows. It slicked his creases. It trickled from tight-shut eyes.

It's the descent or the oven, Fallon thought after a minute. Realistically, all jitters aside, if he made it, say, halfway, even three-quarters, before slipping, odds were he'd survive. Right? But staying up here, in this heat, with not even a drop to grease his pipes...

He swayed to a crouch, teetered 'til the nausea simmered. When he was fairly sure his guts'd stay where they belonged, he crab-walked to the alcove's crook and scooped the egg. 'Sorry about this,' he said, shuffling toward the ledge, wondering if he should lob the thing or simply let go to judge the drop.

Straight plummet, he figured. *See how many outcrops she clips on the way...*

Breathing hard, Fallon sank to his knees, looked down—and howled.

'Quit yer bleating,' Ril called, no more than twenty feet below. 'I still got at least five minutes on the clock.'

Fallon palmed away tears, then scooted back to make room for Ril. In no time, the other lad's long fingers had hooked the ledge. A dirty bandanna came next, then broad shoulders, enviable arms. Nostrils flared, Ril sucked in sour air. His dark eyes were red-rimmed, wild.

'Well then,' Fallon said, grinning. 'Aren't you a right pretty mate.'

'Can't say the same for yerself.' The joke quavered, fell flat as Ril's nervous smile. 'But now that I'm here, reckon I'll take ya.'

'Will you now,' Fallon said, chuckling.

No quick retort.

'Yeah,' Ril said at last, voice trembling. 'Reckon I will.'

'Mate,' Fallon repeated. There was nothing more to say. This was Ril's one shot, and he'd grabbed it. No hesitation. Never worrying about the fall.

He extended a hand.

Carefully, Fallon took it.

The foghorn boomed.

ANOTHER MOUTH

Maura has no beef or blood pudding to offer when the young strangers come knocking. No mackerel, no lamprey, no lamb. They won't take stale bread, or fish heads, or chard, but sometimes, *sometimes* they'll take dairy. Before daybreak she drained Old Bess's udders, half-filling a small tin pail. At dusk she placed saucers of milk on the stoop, laced with arsenic and lye—but poor Nally had quickly lapped it all up, poor, poor little kitten, too hungry to know he was eating death.

'Tomorrow,' she calls now, while knuckles rap-tap outside in the dark. Her husband sits at table, not quite drooling; a glisten pooled on his lip. Eyes on the door, Maura edges closer to him. She reaches down absentmindedly. Smooths his thinning hair with her palm. Scrubs his slack mouth with her sleeve. She whips a bib from her apron pocket, fastens it around Michael's neck. There was a time he'd have whacked the scrap of cloth from her hands, with Barrel looking on and snotty-nosed laughing. There was a time he'd have belted her right then and there, for picking and poking and fussing. For treating him like a child.

Michael was well-salted, well-roughed by the sea; his temper sharp as his pride. When they were alone, he was often gentle. Kissing Maura's bruises. Pulling out when she said so. Drinking whiskey watered with ice. But in sight of his crew—the foster boy, mostly—he was, first and foremost, a captain.

Not so long ago, he'd have cuffed his own spitty beard, thank you, Maura. He'd have worn the brine like a medal.

Soot clouds from the fireplace as young strangers top the roof, plugging the chimney with cold feet and arses. Others run round the house, hammering clapboards with twiggy fingers. Kicking the foundations. Rattling shutters.

'Tomorrow,' Maura shouts, hoping they'll hear. Hoping they'll listen. She has nothing but words to appease them. 'We've none to spare tonight—not a lick—but the lad'll haul in a big catch come morning.'

Liar, knock the young strangers with cartilage and bone.

Liar, rages the wind off the ocean, hissing with Barrel's voice.

Their luck had been fine before the boy came.

Sure, their rent was in arrears. And, sure, the fishing was dire. Most nights, Michael sailed out at moondark; most dawns he sailed in with nets empty. At sea, his harpoon was ever-primed, the blade and hook sharp, the rope strong. They hadn't seen a decent-sized whale in months. Defiant, Michael scoured the beaches for shellfish. Pants rolled to the knees, he'd hunted the shallows, poking a long cruel stick into holes in the sand. But when the tides went out, the shores were often bare. No cockles, no mussels, no clams.

Twice a week Maura went and cooked other folks' meals, stirring up feasts from their plenty. She'd sip the sauces she made, taste the stews for seasoning, dip into the vats of butter she'd churned. The barons generously complimented her skills—*Where'd you get this lass*, they'd boom at their hosts. *Only seventeen! So many years of good cooking ahead of her!*—and they'd hire her for an evening, for a week, for a pittance.

Stomach rumbling, Maura left their lavish dining rooms and pocketed leftover strips of bacon. Balls of suet. Roasted potatoes. Shortcakes. Satchel heavy with pilferings, she'd leave their warm houses with a few extra pennies, but scarcely a crumb for herself.

On the way home, she'd buy a fistful of corned beef, some salted pork or a couple of hocks. The meat went into the soup pot with onions and cabbage; the rest went outside for the strangers.

Keep things as they are, she'd whisper, lining windowsills and doorstep with offerings. *We'll make do, we'll be fine. If it's just us two. Together. Alone.*

Maybe the bacon had gone off that long-ago night.

Maybe the cakes were rancid.

Maybe the young ones were sick of potatoes.

The next morning, the leavings were all gone—and so, it seemed, was her luck.

For the first six months of his life, the boy's name had been Darryl. After his da, so the parish priest said. Clad in mourning black, wide brim drooping in the rain, the old Father was a sorry mess. Part of his act, Maura now thinks; but at the time, he put on such a good show none but God Himself could tell where the truth ended and the lies began. Wilting on their doorstep, the priest stood there sniffling and coughing in his threadbare cassock, begging Christian charity. His arms too scrawny to carry the swaddled thing as far as he had, over paddocks and bogs to the seaside—and much, much too scrawny to lug it all the way back.

Have a heart, he said, *for this miracle child.* Its parents lost in the drink, their ship run afoul, and no survivors but this one tiny bub. *Just like Moses*, he claimed. *An innocent boy set adrift in a basket, lost but now found, now wanting protection. Needing a kind soul to take him in.*

Give it here. Breath whooshed from Maura's belly as she hoisted the creature across the threshold. *No wonder it's squalling. You're squeezing its guts in two.*

Bless you, daughter, the priest sighed, shaking the feeling back into his arms, groaning and stretching his back. *You'll be a good Ma, girl. Mark my words.*

No, she replied, looking down at the bub, his round face like a well-slapped backside. He was solid, even then. A two-gallon keg wriggling in Maura's embrace, overfull and sloshing.

No, she said. *We won't have him.*

It was a simple decision: the *only* decision. Haddock and cod had only just started spawning. They'd only smoked enough herring to see them through spring, much less summer, fall and winter. There were only so many manor houses in this county—and Maura's pockets were only so big. To her mind, there were no ifs, ands or buts about it. Michael was her one and only. They wouldn't have a child.

Then Michael cleared his throat.

Business will never expand without more hands on deck, he said, forgetting that with extra hands came extra mouths. *And you've said yourself that a helpmeet wouldn't go astray.*

But this one's a barrel, *Michael.*

Well now, he said, chest swelling. *That he is.*

After a few noisy minutes, the ruckus on the roof peters out. The windows shudder once, twice more and finally go still. Maura's shoulders relax. Her pulse slows. Once her hands stop shaking, she ladles weak broth into a bowl. As Michael stares, she mixes in their last dollop of lard, dragging a spoon quietly through the liquid. Barely making a ripple. Careful not to spill a drop, not to splash.

Ever since Barrel followed his parents into the deeps, Michael's shied from anything wetter than tears. He won't bathe, won't wash the salt from his face or damp the dried scales from his hands. A fortnight has passed since the boy's drowning; now the cottage reeks of sorrow and rotten fish. Fourteen days' worth of musk, sour cheese, and guilt have fouled the small space, fourteen rank layers for each year of Barrel's short life. Sitting at table, day in and out, Michael wallows in the stench of regret. Dwindling from the bold whale-hunter Maura still loves into a worn-out, one-flue harpoon. Eating only what Maura can coax down his throat, drinking barely enough to stop crumbling.

For two weeks, the same routine. Not long after sundown, Maura guides him from table to bed. Kisses his oily forehead, strokes his lank hair. Starlight silvers the room when she snuffs the lamp, glinting off Michael's unblinking eyes. She sleeps beside him, despite the stink.

Holding him close. Breathing his breath. At moondark she gets up with him. Gathers his gear. Opens the front door. Waits for him to head out.

Two weeks and he's gone no further than the table. Clutching the frayed rope twisted round his paunch. The lifeline that failed to bring his son home.

Hating to leave—Michael's grief, she thinks, is too dangerous—Maura takes little work. The festive season has passed; now landlords and wives are stuffed in their dens, hibernating until the crocuses bloom. Forced to live off their blubber, the barons keep a close eye on their winter larders. When she can, Maura filches onions or fried fat, a turnip for Michael's dinner. Always, she bags rat-bait for the young strangers.

'Almost ready,' she says now, adding a coin of stale bread to the soup. Thumbing up crumbs, she listens for rap-tapping at shutters and door, listens for Barrel's howl. She puts her thumb to Michael's mouth, wipes. The crumbs sit like sand on his tongue.

'I miss him, too,' she says, convincing no one. Michael blinks. Breathes in and out. Makes no reply. Settling into the seat beside him, Maura's mind drifts. The young strangers have never been good to them. Brought them together, sure, and saw them married to boot. But that isn't enough to keep him, is it? That isn't enough to bring him back. She watches the bread bloat with soup and thinks about Barrel. Underwater, somewhere. His broad torso swollen to bursting. Limbs greened with seaweed. Blued muscles disintegrating, a buffet for sardines.

That's what Michael wants, she thinks. What he's always wanted.

Someone beside him, out on the waves.

Someone to raise.

Someone more than her.

Nowadays Maura feeds her husband the way he did Barrel before the boy learned to bite. Spoonful after spoonful, shovelling it in, scraping off the excess. Humming a little tune to keep him calm. Prattling between ditties, saying nothing much. 'How's that, love? Is that good?

Mmmm, you're hungry today, aren't you?' With each gulp, she wishes he'd bark at her, say she's scalded the roof of his mouth. She wishes he'd call her a ninny. Wishes he'd laugh.

'Think you can manage this?' She presses the spoon into Michael's limp hand, knowing how angry he'll be to find his calluses all softening, the leather-hard palm turning to silk. Bending his fingers around the handle, she guides his arm through the motions—dip, lift, slurp, dip, lift, slurp—until he follows through on his own.

'Good work, love,' she says, hearing a scratch of claws at the door. 'Keep going.'

Michael smacks and slobbers while Maura gets up to let in the cat. 'Good work,' she repeats, watching him as she unbolts the lock. Then she turns and swings the door wide. Cooing *here, puss-puss*, she looks outside. To her left and right, yellow lines fall through the shutters and glow in thin rows across trampled grass. A long rectangle stretches from Maura's feet, outlining her silhouette in gold on the path. Vision strained in the darkness, she spots lanterns dotting the valley. Lamps bobbing on masts in the harbour. The moon flickering through scudding clouds. 'Hungry, m'lad?' she asks, stepping aside. 'Come on, then. In you get.'

Fresh air blows into the cottage, crisp with seaweed and salt, cool with spray. It cuts through the room's fug, clearing Maura's head.

She shivers.

And gasps.

And remembers.

Poor, poor Nally.

White-crested waves crash on the coast as the young stranger creeps up the stairs. With arctic tread it slips into the house, shoeless and solemn and pale. Its trousers rolled above the ankle, sleeves above the wrists. Scalloped buttons carved of shell run the length of its arms, grazing Maura's belly as it slinks past. She shudders at the creature's touch, light though it is, somehow more feather than flesh.

Before pulling up a chair at the table, the wight glances at Maura. Nods with an almost imperceptible tilt of its chin.

Yes, she reads in that gesture. *I am hungry*.

Wherever there's fear, Maura's da used to say, there's usually hope.

Ignoring her instincts, she doesn't scream, doesn't shove the stranger right back outside. Instead, she closes the door. Edges around the table. Serves it a small cupful of broth. Praying for luck, she watches the thing gulp it all down. Steam curls from its nostrils, mouth squelching and gaping for more. Maura holds her breath as Michael's bloodshot eyes flick up, meeting clear white. Fear, she thinks. And hope. The creature is nothing like Barrel—grey and lean where the other was ruddy and squat—but sitting where it is, in the boy's long-cold seat, it just might catch her husband's interest. It might just reel him back.

Reaching over, the young stranger pries open Michael's jaw. With long, long fingers it scrapes sadness off his tastebuds and cheeks, then sucks its digits clean. Michael sags, all his fight lost at sea. His dark gaze drops, his focus once more submerged. He leaves his mouth open for plunder.

'Wake up,' Maura hisses. 'Do something!'

Resuming its cycle—dip, lift, slurp, dip, lift, slurp—the spoon clinks against pottery and teeth. Smiling, the wight burrows lower, gouging straight into Michael's belly. Snagging every misery-soaked morsel he's swallowed. Digging with such speed, its nails don't leave a mark, don't even rip the grease-stained shirt. In and out, quick as life. Water burbles from Michael's throat.

The thing grins beside him, chewing the half-mashed sop in its hand.

'We've given all we can,' Maura says, trying her damnedest to be polite. Hypocritical boors, the young strangers demand courtesy—no matter how badly they've skimped on the luck. It's one thing to poison their snacks for a fortnight, another altogether to banish them from the table they'd won her. Maura knows plagues are incited in such ways. Children stolen. Whole families burnt to death in their houses.

'Leave him alone.' she says. Then, recalling what tricksters strangers are with words, she clarifies: 'Please. Let us be alone, together.'

The creature cocks an eyebrow, its smile growing. Maura runs through her request, looks at it backwards and front. *Let us be alone...*

Together alone... Together. Nodding, the thing chortles. *Yes*, its grimace says. *Together, together, together.* Ploughing into Michael's stomach, it gorges, hollowing him out. Solidifying as it eats. Bite after bite, it shrinks; first to half its size, then half that again. Small but not wan and flimsy; small but robust, a parcel too heavy to lug very far. Condensing, compacting, it pinks like a pig, the chair groaning beneath its new weight. Only its fingers remained unchanged: twice as long as Maura's own, insidious as smoke, they scour and hook and latch.

'Enough,' Maura says, cracking the thing's knuckles with her ladle, the way she used to Barrel's when he was greedy. Fool, she thinks immediately, guts twisting. Already she smells the cottage in cinders around them. Any minute, deadly pustules will bulge from her limbs. And Michael. Poor, poor Michael. The husband she'd bought with meat and tears—one glutton consumes his mind, another devours his body. Soon he'll be nothing but skin, hair and bones. And soon Maura will be left alone, as she'd asked, though not at all as she wanted. It won't be her and Michael, alone together. There will just be her, just Maura. Alone with a stranger.

Unless she can steal what her husband needs most.

Unless she can steal them a future.

'That's enough,' she says, to Michael this time, prising the spoon from his grip. 'We mustn't leave our guest out.' Broth dribbles down his chest, a streak so dark and wet it makes him weep. As he snuffles into his salt-crusted beard, Maura reaches for his bowl and swigs what's left of the soup.

Watching intently, the creature sniffs. Its fingers slide out of Michael's stomach. Blank eyes track Maura's every movement. Trailing her as she skirts then sits on the opposite side of the table. Squinting at the black pot cooling on a trivet beside her. Tracing the line of her hands as they lift the cast-iron crock to her mouth.

Maura drinks deep, determined this offering will be her last.

This promised gutful.

Amplified inside the pot, her breathing obscures the sound of bare feet shuffling closer. Chair legs scrape on the stone floor as the young stranger squeezes in beside her. Grunting and wheezing, it clambers up, the woven-straw seat squeaking as the thing leans over. Slowly, deftly, its fingers strum her belly like a lute. Maura jumps at the ice in its touch, the scritch of sharp nails against her apron. Inhaling a lungful, she sputters and coughs. A tongue laps up what's spilled, licking her neck.

When her throat clears, Maura begins humming between swallows. A soft, soothing song—one of Barrel's favourites—with sleepy, familiar lilts. Soon, Michael's weeping subsides, but the clawing at her guts persists. Pausing to drink down the soup's dregs, Maura steadies herself. Then, humming louder and stronger, she peeks at the barnacle suckling her middle. Buried up to the elbows, it's now shrivelled blue-white. Compact as a roast ham. Fat cheeks clotted as though smeared with soft cheese. Slopping liquid into its purple maw, it gazes up at her and sighs.

Together, it purrs. Alone together.

'How's that, love?' Maura says. 'Is that good? Mmmm, you're hungry today, aren't you?'

And as it nods, Maura brings the pot cracking down, then rams the stunned head face-first inside her. Grabbing the thing's pudgy rump, she *shoves*. Her innards writhe and compress, but she won't stop—no, she won't be alone. Bladder leaking through her cotton skirt, she jams tiny arms up under her ribcage and legs down into her pelvis. She pushes and grunts, pushes and grunts, until all that remains are the creature's clawed toes, wriggling from a black gap in her navel.

'There now,' she says, mashing its feet out of sight, leaving no mark on her apron, no gash. Full of promise, the squirmer spins inside her. Full of raw luck, Maura reaches for Michael's hand. Presses it against the full moon of her belly.

'Look what I've got for you,' she says to her man. 'Extra hands, love. Another mouth.'

Lacing her fingers through his, she rubs the taut fabric curved between breasts and lap. Together, their palms shush back and forth like the tide. Together, Michael's eyes focus as little heels kick and little elbows jab. Together, their chests swell.

THE HONEY STOMACH

We promised not to eat you.

Fate-bound and honest, we promised, though you came out like a fancy treat on Ma Clary's dessert cart, a rare confection folk like us only ever glimpsed through the thin domes of her crystal cake stands. A delicate surprise.

Oh sure, we were expecting—nine full moons had drowned in the sea since we'd seen the first signs of your quickening—

but we thought you'd arrive red and rough and squalling. Rugged, like us. Built for rowing, hauling nets, standing for endless hours on the gutting stage, welts stinging from wrists to elbows and knuckles crusted with salt, squid-ink gloves clenched on your knife's scum-slicked handle. We thought you'd be solid. That you'd put up a fight.

But a pang and a push at the breakfast table was all it took. A slurp and a slop. Before Doc Peddle hupped that black bag of his in through the parlour, there you were. Small and lumpy as a figgy duff, your skin a clear wobble of gelatin and your little limbs riddled with holes. Rum-raisin eyes taking us in. A whiff of sponge toffee in your cries.

Oh, how our poor bellies rumbled.

Its organs are intact and all parts are accounted for, Doc told us, reassuring for only a second. *But the muscles are a right royal mess.*

Haven't seen the like in years, if I'm honest, not since Naddy Calhoon birthed her own—and he hesitates then, wraps his head around the odds of such a fluke striking twice in our lifetime—*honeycomb bairn*. We let that sink in, the three of us, watching sugar water pump through your veins. More hummingbird food than blood.

The lungs won't last long, he said. *Best say your farewells while its yet alert. After that's up to you. Leave it out on the sill for the young strangers. Take it to the glade for the moss-kin, if you're that way inclined. Anyroad, I'll give old Kellaway a call. Order up a keg of his finest black for the wake.*

Never mind him, we whispered. Doc Peddle's a known quack.

You came to us for a reason, we thought. Who would throw such a blessing away?

You survived that day.

The next.

And the next.

Our skiff was docked for months while we learned how to tend you. Salt-herring fed us the while, and what knobbled roots we'd stored in the cold cellar, along with the goodness our neighbours spared from their own larders: cheese and hard tack that kept us from starving in the leanest of weeks. We'd never known such hunger.

Never thought we'd ever know worse.

Who could blame us for kissing your honeyed tears? Absent-mindedly licking our fingers after squeezing you into flannel sleep-sacks? Wiping nectar from your gummy eyelids and stirring it into our thrice-boiled tea? Not a soul on this rock. These were sweet nothings. Innocent offerings. Little gifts that uplifted us—like your smiles, your burbled songs—all the sap of your joys and sorrows. A peck on your sticky cheek sustained us for days.

We swore not to sup any deeper.

Suddenly you outlived an entire groundfishing season. An ice harvest. Another whole turn of the sun's wheel. Soon you were somewhat upright, yammering at us from first to last light, more animated than any of the travellers' world-renowned puppets. Around about then, our hound nipped off two of your toes—the biggest one and the tallest—and, oh, what a fright it gave us! Quiet with shock, you wide-eyed the syrup oozing red gold from the stubs, while we hollered at the rotten mutt and strung driftspinner's amulets around your ankles and feet, brass-and-shell charms bespelled to summon bees. Quack Peddle was useless, we thought. Let nature provide what mainland science can't. In time, the drones hummed on over here to help, sealing up nubs and reshaping that what the retriever had swallowed. Even now, that bloody dog's never looked more hale. Nary a hitch in his sprint nor a grey whisker on his old muzzle.

And then somehow, you were three. Four. Five. Sharp as a jig hook, even back then—and with such a memory! You tallied every sardine in the tin, recalling every which crock of whey that was empty, every which bottle of milk was half-full. You divvied your share of the stew, scraping some aside for the strangers, some for the mutt, some for one or both of us to find on chilly evenings when we got back home from a poor day's baiting. Oh, you snarfled the gumdrops Saint Nick left in your bucket on snowday mornings, but usually you gave us a taste too. Always, we only bit what was ours to chew.

Even when the sea was stingy.

Even when our very souls ached with want.

We thought the bees would've left by now, migrated to fresher flowers, but we can't say we minded the care they took of you. The Queens ruling the hives in your heart, head, and belly, their subjects knitting wounds, they all buzzed you bigger and stronger each year. They rebuilt what was lost, broken.

Oh, the questions you concocted while they worked! So many wheres and whys and hows that we'd not so much as fathom ourselves in a dog's age: *why don't they sting me* and *what does feast mean* and *how do yolks get inside eggs* and *will you die one day? Will I?*

We answered truthful, always, even to that.

Not for a long time, we replied with great hope. And if God's good you'll live even longer than that.

By six, your Stagg blood simply *bayed* for far-travels. Though not actually walking—not then, not ever—you were mobile enough in that carry-cart we crafted for you. That upturned wicker skep, still fixed to its squeaky wheels, did a fine job of containing your wee waxen limbs. Collecting what honey we might otherwise miss.

(We only consumed the dregs. The drips. The bits that crumbled off on their own. Sloughed hair and skin. Productive sneezes. Fingertips accidentally pinched in the door. Not a gulp more.)

The short roll from our hut to the harbour wasn't adventure enough for you. Not once you'd grown so hearty. Few foreign hulls shuddered against the grand pier by then, few mermaids launched their schooners there, few booths lifted their awnings in the quay markets. The bicker and beck of our rollicking bay lost its appeal when the cod started playing silly buggers, refusing to school into our nets as they once did, hoarding their rich silver shoals elsewhere instead. Up and up, we pushed your barrow along paths suddenly more scree than meadow. The beaches behind us retreated like an ancient crone's gums. No clams left to dig down there, no skua nests to raid in the cliffs, only miles of barren waters. Harsh winters had sheared once-lush hillsides like greedy stockmen, their blades gouging fast, heedlessly cutting before tearing their bounty away. Stunted trees clung to thin soil. Only the hardiest greens sprouted from stone-seeded gardens. Few blossoms supported your swarms.

Around your bright flaxen head, the poor bees' numbers shrank like our own bellies. You were down to one Queen. A tiny court of her most devoted servants. The syrupy swill in your core wouldn't nourish half that many.

We wheeled over to the town square next—as you insisted—to see the holly boughs swooping in berried chains above the cobbles. The jolly merchants and their shimmer-glass shopfronts. The brazier-b'ys serving up spit-roasted snacks to children with coins jangling in pouches and pockets, kids who could run home to their kin with grease on their faces and shoes on their reliable feet.

What happened, you asked as we rattled through near-empty

courtyards. A bee whizzed out of your ear, zigzagged over battened stalls and up to slate-shingled rooftops, disappearing into the afternoon glare. *Where is everyone?*

We thumbed the golden globs welling between your brows, sucked on that sugar while framing the truth as we know it, facts to fit the sweetest hollows of your heart. Some folk have it even worse than us, we said. Hex-singers and driftspinners won't change a family's fortunes for free. Young strangers won't be tempted with dried curds and crusts. In this life, we said, you got to give if you want to receive. No matter where that leaves you. No matter the cost.

That's what they've done, we told you, clattering past Scattergood's unshuttered windows. Inside, the baker swept his young daughters toward the front door, apron hanging loose round his middle as he pushed the broom behind them. At the counter, his once-pudgy wife was awfully gaunt. The girls giggled into the yard. Mirth soon gave way to exhaustion. On a patch of dry grass between the street and the shop, they sat and spun tales of distant lands hidden in gaps between the sun's rays.

These folk have given their all to this world, we said. Now they're shoring their strength. Waiting for luck's tide to turn.

Your voice is light as you beckon the lasses over.

Let me give you something to eat, you said, holding out your empty hand. *I've got plenty.*

Confused, the girls shuffle closer.

Is this some sort of trick?

Just this once, we said, palms suddenly damp and pulse choking-fast.

Just a bite, we said.

Bees circled your crown, flying in a fuzzed frenzy. All these years, they haven't stung any one of us. Not even once.

It's okay. Nectar seeped from your dear, crooked smile, and good gods how it made our chests swell! Oh, how we love you, our sweet surprise. Our honey stomach. *It doesn't hurt.*

Just one bite, we repeated. We promise.

Just like this, we said as you nodded, before turning to the children. Showing them how it's done.

THE ESCAPE

Scattergood's bakery is the only place in Churnsey Bay with fine leaded windows. Up Ballyhack Hill way, all the two-storey houses glint and glimmer with glass—those rich merchant-mariners love sneering at the village below through long perfect casements, each clear as a crisp winter morning—but down here in the windy cove most shops have one or two portholes at best, small circles with chipped and salt-rimed glazing. Closer to the harbour, fishmongers' booths aren't even that lucky. Little but glorified timber frames, their stalls are open-faced and open-sided to vent the wares' stink, lengths of waxed sealskin and canvas furled on the transoms, ready to buffer the worst of the weather. Over on Frillwater Flat, the Orr brothers' smithy boasts a lone skylight in its shingled roof —but the forge, braziers, and wide-flung barn doors do plenty to brighten their humble workshop. All over the Rock's sand-swept inlet, clapboard cabins squat with single candle-lit windows winking beside their front doors. Unshuttered, warm, welcoming.

But the bakery—housed in a cobblestone cottage that's been in the family since Chance Scattergood dropped anchor here two-hundred-odd years ago—has three of them. Three! Enormous things, each taller than Emmaline with her thick arms upraised and twice again that broad, they shine from knee level up to the eaves, enclosing the storefront in a dazzle of harlequin crystal.

Magic, Aegis Scattergood thinks, hovering in the pink gleam of dawn trapped in their magnificent, faceted glass. *Pure magic.*

She can only guess what swindle Chance might've swung to nab such a rare treasure, but *who* the old crook got it from is no mystery. Not to her. When they were little, she and Emmaline often curled like kittens on the shop's maple floor, drowsing away the late afternoon lull before closing time. While their Da mangled sweetbreads for savory pies and Mither whipped honey butter to make breakfast rolls, Em dreamed in the drowsy light of sundown, oblivious to the horde of slender fingers slinking through the red-orange beams, tickling Aegis's sides 'til she cackled.

Looking in from the strangers' side of things, Aegis secretly watches her sister hup tray after tray of balled dough into the proofer. It's too dark out yet for her to shimmer through the eastern window into the kitchen, so she loiters in the gloaming while Emmaline ripples across the whitewashed room, her movements warped by the wrinkles between worlds. Em has never seen these brightways between realms, never stepped slantwards through rays of fae-filtered light—much less ridden their dawn-shafts and dusk-slides, as Aegis so often does, to cavort with the good folk in their otherlands—nor connected such seeings and steppings with the bakehouse's marvellous windows. Em is too practical for such mysteries. Too busy to notice them. Too tired.

Aegis's stomach rumbles, but Em can't hear it. In the morn's rising glow, she swings the hot-box's heavy doors shut. Sets a timer. Stokes the big oven's fire. She hauls sacks of millet and mixed seeds out of a low cupboard, thumps them onto a floured workbench, scoops handfuls onto unleavened rounds. While the bannocks brown, she preps the day's currant buns, gooseberry tarts, fruitcakes, sunflower muffins. Aegis smiles at her sister's focus. Her day-to-dayness. Her salt-of-the-earthness. She's solid as brandywine pudding, is Em. Wholesome as a loaf of dark rye.

Everything Aegis is not.

Pins-and-needles prickle her from nose to toes as the sun rises from a dull pewter sea. She prods the barrier between realms with a withy-spindle staff, testing for possible passage points: it *stretches* around the knobbled wood like a sheet of warm butterscotch, but doesn't yet yield.

On the other side, Emmaline dashes into the back room to fetch a kerchief. Hurries out again. Knots the calico around her molasses curls. Yesterday's bagged leftovers go on the counter—a penny a piece or three for two cents—before she tops up the pyramid of marmalades and jams. A baby mewls in the loft above the shop, a thin hungry cry that can't be ignored for long. Em flips the flatbreads first then darts into the pantry, grabs a bottle of fresh buttermilk, and creaks up a narrow flight to the Scattergood family home. Within seconds, three high voices pip at their mam. Little feet thunder behind the chimney while she coos and sings and feeds her youngest. Downstairs, the timer jangles.

Watch your brother, Aegis hears from afar, *keep him upright if he's gassy*, and Em wavers back down to work.

Now the trays come out of the proofer. One by one, Emmaline braces them atop the latest nine-month swell of her belly, swings round, shunts the raw loaves onto roasting stones and into the oven. A clunk and thump overhead set the oil lamps a-swaying and a girl's holler wails through the ceiling.

'Everyone alive?' Em calls up, reaching for the same charred wooden paddle their Da's own palms polished smooth. Out comes the bannock, in go the pastries. She cuffs soot and sweat from her broad face.

Yes, Mither! But Dancey's hogging the jitterbugs—

Am not—

'Deal with it,' Emmaline shouts, and there's a weariness in her tone that Aegis doesn't much like, a shrillness Em clearly regrets. Wincing, she crosses her arms for a second. Rubs the sharp words from her lips. Scowls at the handcrafted calendar marking the weeks until Hender returns. Five months he's been on the waves. Five more to go. With a sigh, she scrawls a line across today's square. It's the first thing the bairns check in the morning, this sea-wife's tally of hope.

Aegis is itching like a good thing now, her walking stick *stretching* dawnlight like blown glass. Another minute or two and she'll be in.

Emmaline takes off her apron as a cabin-shaped clock cuckoos on the wall. She plates the pastries, pops the kids' oats on the hob along with a black kettle for tea. Safe beneath the counter, the lead coffer squeaks open, the coin purse Em withdraws near-silent as she knots it onto her overstretched belt.

'Breakfast,' she shouts up the stairs. Four bowls of porridge clunk on a small table beside the front door. Em straightens with a groan. Knuckles her lower back. Dabs her damp eyes with the heel of her hand. She should flip the sign to *open* now.

She should.

Daybreak streaks into Scattergood's.

'Let me help, Em.' The butt of Aegis's staff thunks on the hardwood floor. She shakes off the tingle of crossing. Static crackles through the great mass of her silver braids, chiming the glass. '*Please*,' she says. 'You need a good break.'

'It'll be fine,' Aegis says. 'It's not that hard.'

She swirls cinnamon and honey into her oatmeal, inhaling the sweet-spicy scent. Each spoonful is bliss. No one else has Emmaline's knack for good hearty fare, least of all Aegis; one of many reasons Em inherited their folks' trade while *she* headed down Barradoon way to set up a life she could own. She adds a splash of cream, savours every mouthful. Not like the bairns, those ravenous hellions, who'd scooped, slopped and slurped their bowls empty before tumbling outside to play. Two b'ys and two girls shriek in the yard—a pair of copper-haired twinsets in coveralls and crewnecks, roughhousing like pups—while the youngest bub naps upstairs in her cot. Five kids under seven and another almost fully cooked. Too many for one mam to manage. All the time. On her own.

'It's just a little respite,' Aegis says, scraping the dregs from her dish. The bell jangles as Quinnie Croft bustles in for her ha'penny loaf. The door's springs are shot; salt air sweeps in behind her, cutting a cold path through the bakery's malt-and-yeast balm. Gulls cry for lost mates in the village square. Through the south window, Aegis spies Thom and Jape wielding branches like swords, thrashing the birds out to sea. Em takes the seamstress's coin, nods her thanks, and flinches as the door bangs shut. Dishcloth in hand, she wipes invisible crumbs off the pastry case. Fetches the black-boiler and a new teabag. Refreshes her sister's pot.

'*Sit*, woman.' Aegis thumps the tabletop and glares until she relents. Emmaline trivets the kettle and pulls a chair all the way out, huffing as she lowers herself onto its quilted cushion. Her gaze drops to the worn scrap of cotton in her lap. She folds and unfolds and refolds it. Not looking at Aegis, but *listening*.

'I'm no mither, but I can handle the wee monsters for one night,' Aegis says calmly, as if she hasn't pitched this idea a dozen times since Mabel arrived, persuading with patience rather than pressure. 'We'll get them fed, tuck them in tight, then slip down to catch the eventide exchange. I'll whisk you through the west window and be back here in a blink, ready to deal with their nightmares and nappies. And I'll come collect you at cock's crow, I promise. I'll be over with the first shaft of sunrise. Just think on it, Em: you'll have a week to yourself while the bairns are asleep. It'll only be a single night to them—but *six* restful ones for you. Imagine how much better you'll feel then! Trust me, okay? They won't even know to miss you.'

Frowning, Emmaline picks at an old scorch mark on her wrist. Her belly undulates as the baby rolls over. 'I don't know, Aggie,' she says at last. Guilt wars with exhaustion. 'Who'll get the oven going in the morning?' Aegis rolls her eyes, the only response this flimsy excuse warrants. Sure, she's a driftspinner whose hearth-time is mostly spent brewing philtres and potions, conjuring charms to console and to conquer, weaving this and the otherworld's magic—but she still knows her way around the Scattergood kitchen. She'll never forget where she came from.

Emmaline changes tack. 'Won't the young strangers take issue with me gallivanting around their hills for a week?'

Aegis cackles at the thought of her beautiful behemoth of a sister *gallivanting* anywhere these days, but resists the urge to tease. 'Relax, Em. We'll follow the rules. The young strangers *are* particular about who comes and goes—they don't want just *anyone* running roughshod in their territories, you're right about that—but I'm no mere mortal. I'm allowed to bring a guest.' She winks. Grins. Reaches a weathered hand across the table and places it atop Emmaline's plump pink one.

Ignoring the crick in her spine, Aegis leans in. Lowers her chin to meet Em's eyes. Lets her take in the tarnished silver of her hair, her age spots and wrinkles—signs of what she's sacrificed to *that* realm. The weeks she's lost here for the decades she's lived there. The price of striding the brightways, exploring the otherlands, meeting and learning from the fae folk. Taking not a whit more than they deigned to give.

Now Aegis is much, *much* more ancient than her young, older sister. Much wiser.

'You need this, Em.'

'Are you sure it'll work?' Emmaline's voice is quiet, considering. 'Have you even done this before?'

'The only thing I know better than the sunways is *you*, me ducky. I'll get you there.'

Once more, the bell jingles. In limps Garrup Orr, moaning and complaining about the rot in his boot as he clomps to the counter, pausing only to paw at the mound of Em's belly—*My Credence never looked half so worn out with child as you, lass*—as she *oofs* herself up to serve him. A cob of pumpernickel and two sweetbuns later, Garrup's carrying his coal-stink outside, barking road-hockey advice at the b'ys. The latch clicks behind him, shutting out the slap of hornbeam sticks on hard leather balls, the lads' whines and the girls' cheers as Dancey's team scores.

Behind the counter, Em slips a cold coin into her pouch. Yawns. Points her face at the great windows. Gazes inward. 'What would Hender say?'

Aegis clenches her jaw. Breathes hard out her nose.

'You'll be back long before he is,' she says.

Interference! Get in the penalty box, Jape! A brawl breaks out in the yard. High-pitched curses screech into howls. *Mam! Thom's cheating!* Upstairs, Mabel starts to bawl.

For half a second—a good hour in the otherworld—Emmaline wilts.

'Just one night?'

Aegis smiles. 'Just one.'

They shine westwards a few minutes shy of nightfall. As Aegis promised, they'd stuffed the kids sleepy, snugged them abed and then snuck down to the shop, followed by milky snuffles and gentle, stew-bellied snores. After filling one basket with sourdough, hard cheese, butter, nuts and dried fruit, and another with jars of fresh water—*don't eat what they offer*, Aegis said, *no matter how tempting*—they shouldered duffels stuffed with cloaks and winter-wool dresses.

'Hold tight,' Aegis says and white-knuckles Em's sweaty grip, *pulling* when her heavy feet drag. Despite the sunset's fiery hue, as they step into the brightest stream of light, a sharp chill engulfs them; a frostfall of tickling fingernails. 'Aggie? Is this—'

'Perfectly normal,' she assures, voice light with relief as her thin shoe crunches down on cockleshell gravel. 'Hurry now, let's get you settled. I don't have much time.'

Behind them, the bakery's big diamond-hatched panes are wedged into the broad side of a shaggy grass knoll. Inside, Scattergood's wavers like a gauze curtain in a summer breeze, the clock's pendulum slowed almost to a stop. But out here, the glass reflects the sky's alpenglow hues: pastel washes of magenta, mauve, salmons and faint reds that steep the world in perpetual gloaming. White clover, yarrow, and fluffs of bog cotton twinkle like stardust all over the mound and beyond, sprinkling the wild lawns that roll from the hillside to a ragged brook a stone's throw away, to the deep purple fishing pond nearby, to the willow wood weeping all around them. Birds warble weird watery tunes. Will-o-the-wisps ghost among the flowers. The wind sighs, shushes, demands quiet.

The young strangers keep their peace in the shadows.

Gaping at the view, Emmaline is pink and buttercream, burnished peach. 'I get it now,' she whispers, baskets by her feet, hands resting on her belly. 'How this place has ensnared you.'

The fist clenching Aegis's guts loosens its grip. Smiling, she collects Em's things and nudges her along. A little ways up the path, a traveller's wagon is camped beneath a crabapple tree. Pale blossoms blanket its arched wooden bonnet and the copper chimney sprouting crookedly from it. Small drifts whiten the coach's slim platform and carved railings at its end, petals skimming across the three steps leading down to the ground. Prickle roses and tangleroots tether its spoked wheels to the spot, leaves and flowers sparked with fireflies. Two whittled lanterns swing from an awning above the one narrow door, unlit yet somehow radiant, inviting them in.

'It's not much,' Aegis says, 'but it's clean and the mattress is comfy. Enjoy yourself, me ducky. You deserve it.'

With Em nestled in bed and the sun back home in Churnsey Bay dipping dangerously low, Aegis hotfoots it to the hill and shimmers into the bakery with the day's last flash. Floorboards creak as she pads over to the big brick oven to pile a few slow-burning logs on the coals. The clock ticks steadily as she gives the workbench and counter a once-over with a damp cloth, checks the proofer's water levels, and puts the sourdough bannetons in the cold storage to gently rise overnight. Upstairs, the kids haven't budged. Dancey and Grace lie head-to-toe in one bunk, Thom and Jape sprawl on separate pallets, and wee Mabel stirs in her wicker cot. Aegis sleeps terribly, but the bairns aren't to blame. Twice she has to soothe the baby's red gums with ice cubes and once, at the deepest blue of moondark, she has to guide the girls out to the privy, but she was already awake when they called out to her, after tossing in half-lucid nightmares about labyrinths and ever-shrinking tunnels and tides that simply refused to carry her ship in to shore.

When the first tint of dawn limns the loft's gabled dormer, Aegis is up and lacing her boots, slipping a worn leather vest over her quilted grey tunic, and stuffing a handful of freshwater pearls into her trousers' hip pocket—a modest thank you for the young strangers. Then she's flying downstairs, tapping at the shop's eastern window, testing its give. Too early. She dashes to the oven, stokes it, adds fuel. Runs back to her post. *Tap tap*. Nope. She heats up the stove, fills the kettle, drags a sack of wholemeal flour onto the workbench to save Em's poor back. *Tap tap*. Still hard as arctic ice. Another night without their mam won't kill the children, not with Auntie Aggie around to coddle and crow over them, but Emmaline can't while away another week in the faelands. Aegis paces, *taps*. She can't miss this morning's passage. *Tap tap*.

Come on, she thinks, keeping an ear out for the kids and an eye on the rooftops in the square. At last, the sun rises above the squat row of shingled ridges across the way. Leaning into the light, Aegis breathes through the sting of thorns creeping across her skin, takes a step—and exhales in the lavender haze beyond the hill. The air is damp here today, cold but awfully humid. Shapes burr around the edges. Flowers are inkblots on wet parchment. Trees fuzz into the coral sky. The stream's banks ooze into the sward.

From the corner of her eye, Aegis spies stretched-taffy fingers sliming up out of the pond.

'I'm here, Em,' she calls. 'You ready?'

Her words clunk in the thick air like apples dropped in a barrel. Hustling up the path, she tells herself that Emmaline is dozing. That she's *this* close to bursting with child, so of course she's still tired, even after a week in this twilit getaway. That she's just out behind the wagon, answering nature's call.

'Em?'

On approach, she finds the duffels and panniers they'd brought tossed under the carriage. A fleece-lined cloak spread out on the railing. A bundle of bloodied bedsheets on the landing. Aegis's throat constricts.

'Emmaline?' she croaks, pounding up the steps and through the door. 'Emma—'

'Shhhhhh, we're coming.'

Eyes adjusting to the gloom, Aegis makes out the little potbellied stove to her left. The oak pew to her right a-scattered with small, crocheted cushions. The mismatched shelves for knickknacks and vials. The jute runner leading up to double bed inset in a toll-painted alcove at the wagon's furthest end. There, with the buttons of her blouse mostly undone, her skirts spattered with gods-know what and her hair all mops and brooms, Emmaline sits with a carpet bag hooked on her elbow. One leg dangling over the bedside, the other bent on the blankets, cradling a swaddled babe.

'I'd *just* stepped out the door,' Em says, 'when she yowled for a feed. Thought it best she travel all milk-drunk and dozy instead of wailing like a banshee the whole way. Here, can you take this?'

Aegis frees Em of the carpet bag, helps her stand.

'She's a doll,' she whispers, though the child's pure cocoon from here. Plenty of time to give her a closer look and a squeeze once they're safely away, Aegis thinks. 'Didn't expect her for a while yet—'

'We're fine,' Em says before Aegis can ask. They file out of the caravan, creak down the steps to collect the baskets and bags. 'The pangs came on quick and strong—and so did she! Wee thing knew what she wanted; three pushes and she practically slipped out on her own. Didn't you, my Pip? You gave your mam no trouble at all.'

As Emmaline nuzzles the bub's downy cheek, Aegis steers her back down the path, marvelling at her sister's joy. Her tranquility. Oh, she's got a bird's nest for hair and a sleepless sheen in her eyes, but this weariness is all animal, all muscle and bone, it doesn't haunt her mind, sap her soul. After a week over here, newborn or none, Em is refreshed. Serene.

'Keep her close,' Aegis says as the bakehouse windows invite them home. She bustles in close to Emmaline, luggage clunking and pinching while they lumber up to the sill. Oilslick rainbows quease across the glass, mixing this world's lilac radiance with that one's near-six o'clock gold. Creatures chirrup and scree in the wavering grass. The pondwater blurbs, slurps and sloshes. Shadows flit across the hill's rugged face. For a moment, Aegis's voice grates, overly loud as the otherland inhales, trying to hold onto them a breath longer. 'Your Pip'll bleat a tad on the crossing, but if we hug her between us, we should buffer the worst of its sting—'

'Don't go, Aegis Scattergood,' comes a slurried echo of words behind them. 'After all, you've only just arrived.'

The barbels whiskering the young stranger's wide lipless mouth don't twitch as it speaks. It gloats without effort.

'Break the rules once,' it says, 'shame on you. Break them twice, shame on *me*.' As Aegis turns, she shuffles Em and the baby around behind her, shielding them both from the warden's murkwater gaze. She knows this bitter suckerpunch of a pest all too well; it's been hounding her for a lifetime, set on tricking her, tripping her mid-shimmer, trapping her—once and for all—on the strange side of the hill. More than any other fae she's learned from, listened to, loved or loathed, this one's a separatist: it can't abide earth-steppers, realm-walkers, halfmeasurers like Aegis the Cackler; folk who live here, there, and anywhere. It believes in permanent boundaries. Walls mortared with magic, barricading *us* from *them*.

But it is no ruler, this thin-limbed greyling dripping in algae-knit weeds, this guardian of waterways and windows. It has no retinue, no royal court, no rules of its own—it merely enforces laws brokered by strangers more powerful than it will ever be. Blood oaths sworn with light-striding mortals born and gone long before it first scummed this portal's pond.

It's a petty bureaucrat, Aegis thinks, splitting hairs and slapping wrists to make itself feel strong.

'Save your riddles,' she says, glancing over her shoulder at the brightening shade of morning in Churnsey Bay. 'We've got about a minute before our window closes—'

The thing clicks its thick tongue. Raises a long slug-trail of a finger. 'One guest: that's the rule. One only. Last time, you smuggled in a stowaway. Understand?' Head shaking slowly, it emits a weird *tsk* like spit bubbles snapping, and sludges itself closer. *Closer.* 'This one is ours now.' It leans in to sniff the sweet milky musk of the baby's crown, straightening with a connoisseur's happy sigh. Cold breath wafts between them, a mildewed gust dank with seaweed and worms. 'She stays here.'

'No!' Emmaline shouts. Folding Pip into the hunched cage of her body, she starts hammering at the window. The little panels chime and rattle, but don't yield. '*No!* Aegis! Do somethi—'

The young stranger's arm is a straight spurt of quicksilver shooting past Aegis. Extra-long digits snag the infant before it shoves her mither away. In a burst of red heat and a creak of puddle-ice cracking, Em is through the window. Home.

Gone.

'Look what you've done!' Aegis tilts her head back and howls with mirth but the warden is unruffled, certain as a waystone; it knows what's what. It merely quirks a twiglet brow while she laughs. Pats and jiggles the grizzling child. Shushes her while Aegis rambles.

'Did you mean to hinder us? Trap us here? Ha! This *helps*, don't you see? *You* sent Em across, not *me*—'

Even now, Emmaline is sinking to the shop's timber floor, slow as an ant swimming in honey. It'll be a good quarter of an hour *here* yet before she lands; only a blink over *there*. If Aegis can shine through in the next few minutes, Em won't know the difference... No, no, not *if*: *must*. She'll get Pip and go before this slimalkin slurs another word. She can't—*won't*—let her sister suffer all day, choked with panic, guilt, grief at the thought of Pip lost and alone until dusk reopens the door between realms. A whole week without her mother? Sweet prey for young strangers? No newborn could survive that.

'—so the baby's mine to carry home. Just the two of us, see? No harm, no foul. One traveller, one guest, one crossing. Thanks to you.'

'If you're finished.' The young stranger sways on the spot, gently lulling the child quiet. When she starts rooting for a feed, it slips its thumb into Pip's mouth. As she suckles, it *eels* its neck skywards, extending it by a foot or more, so that its duckweed-slopped head can crane over the bub without disturbing her. 'You can't outtalk the rules, Cackler,' it says between burps and throat convulsions. 'And this is your forfeit for flaunting them. This little soul.'

'No!'

Aegis rushes the creature. Two strides and she's within reach—but she shudders to a stop as the thing points its face groundwards and horks a glob of blue-black phlegm at her feet. With long whelk-knobbled toes, it stirs and scrapes at the muck, whistling as it tamps out a compact mound. A few more deft gouges and four appendages take shape. A stump neck and bulbous head. Now the warden's tune hollows into panflute-like hooting—a powerful wind-summoning, if Aegis ever heard one—and great drifts of air spin to its bidding, carrying seeds and spores and bristling spinnakins, hellebore petals, grey thistledown, clumps of green java moss. Tune and toes stitch them into a patchwork on the spit-darkened soil. Another rheumy gob and the mess smooths out. The limbs and torso straighten. The surface grit slickens to skin.

'This should placate the mother,' the young stranger says, brusque and condescending, but aware Aegis won't stop haranguing it without *some* compromise. The mud-child wriggles while it's poked and prodded, turned this way and that, checked for unwanted cracks, frailties, flaws. Equine features *stretch* then shrink into something less horrid, something almost human. Almost pretty. Liquid black scales on its hindquarters stipple into freckles on olive-toned flesh. Skeins of feathery roots coil into dark hair above a strong brow. Wide brown eyes blink at the marvel of life.

Its maker nods, happy with this work.

'Take it or leave it,' it says to Aegis. 'And *go*.'

Emmaline is not fooled, *not* placated. One whiff and she knows the child is *wrong*.

'Go back,' she begs, blubbering and sniffling, shoving the swaddled thing at Aegis, shoving them both against the eastward glass. 'Please!' Upstairs the bairns are chattering, thunking in and out of bed. Wee Mabel is babbling in her own cheerful language. Down here, the oven's burning low. 'Please, Aggie, go back and get her, get my baby, my Pip, please *go get her*—'

Another hard shove and Aegis's back clunks against the grand window. Her skull cracks on its fine leadwork and the panes ring like crystal windchimes in a gale, but they don't fracture or shatter or *shimmer* her faewards. They don't reopen for any mither's broken-hearted whim. They've survived far worse sorrows than hers.

'I'm sorry, Em.' Aegis cups her sister's hands, presses them tenderly around the moleskin blanket, the tiny changeling asleep in its folds. She's not Pip, that's for sure, but she's not *so* bad. From this angle, Aegis tells herself, she's even cute... 'I'm so sorry. I'll try again tonight, I promise—'

'Stop it,' Emmaline snaps. 'That's enough! Stop talking—*just stop*. I won't hear another word.'

In her arms, the creature startles. Its eyes flick open, irises now thick swirls of jack-tar. The ends of its arms harden into charcoal hooves. The pink flush in its cheeks blackens, grows rubbled and bumped like macadam. Head rearing, its mouth opens. *Whinnies.*

'Look what you've done, Aegis. *You* did this to us, to our sweet babby, our little Pip...' Swallowing a sob, she thrusts the thing away.

Aegis ducks to catch it. 'Curse you! *Take a break, Em. It's just one night, Em. You deserve it, Em*. What am I going to tell Hender? That I lost another one? This far along? Or that she came blue-born—what else can I say?—and now he'll want a proper burial and rites and a shot of salt water, but I can't do anything with *this*, can I?'

'Oh, Em—'

'Get rid of it,' she spits. Above the counter, the cuckoo pops out and retreats, singing six minor notes. An hour until opening. No fresh bread today if Emmaline doesn't get moving. Kind as most folk are 'round the Bay, Scattergood's customers will mourn their own empty bellies more than they will *hers*.

On go her apron and bonnet. Bags and baskets are shunted under the counter and shelves. Heavy sacks of flour and seed are hefted onto the workbench, no problems with her back now, no bulge in her way. 'Grace! Dancey! Get your sister and come down. Boys, your turn to empty the pots!'

'I'll tell them she's mine,' Aegis whispers, lifting the strangeling to her shoulder. 'A new cousin—'

'Don't you dare,' Emmaline says, anger simmering but still hot enough to wound. 'Get out. Now. I never want to see that thing—or you—again.'

'But, Em—'

'Go, Aegis. And don't ever come back.'

Outside, the bakery windows are glaring, impenetrable sheets of reflected sunlight. Hurrying through the square, Aegis glimpses herself in other blank panes, flat yellow circles and blinding white squares; a haggard figure clutching a half-burnt Yule log, not a child, her trouser pockets leaking freshwater pearls. Herring gulls croon her out of town, beckoning her to the Frillwater Flat, the grassy dunes fringing its green marshes, the pitted limestone coast beyond the fenlands. On the wharf, the isle's mermaids are casting off, setting sail to catch bairns of their own, while the town's strongest fishermen are rowing out to wrangle other treasures from the deeps. Bone garlands clatter on the jetty's driftwood posts. Crab shells buzz with gnawed rinds, wind-scoured sweets, broken eggs. Offerings to Rán and her foam-crested daughters. Prayers for good luck. Good findings.

Head down, Aegis avoids the quay market and negotiates the nearby cliff's switchback trail down to the sea. It's about an hour's trek down the coast to Barradoon, a distance she's to-and-froed hundreds of times since trading a baker's burdens for a drift-spinner's liberties. A path she now knows will only ever walk one way. At the very first crunch of her boots on shore, the first gust of salt breezes, the changeling stirs. Nose crinkling, it sniffs the air. Wrinkles its brow into a fish-scaled darkness. Looks out at the waves and starts howling.

'Hush now,' Aegis urges and for an instant the creature obeys. In that brief silence, she contemplates keeping the little thing. The girl. Raising her. Acting the mither. There's room enough in a clapboard hut for two, she thinks, especially with such a wee bub as this one. All she needs is a cot, or even just a foot of Aegis's own mattress, and when she grows into a bed of her own, the joys she'll bring will surely outweigh the lack of space in their cabin. *Imagine the spells we'll craft together, the rune-charms we'll knit, the potions we'll brew for honest folk from Churnsey and Helmswith and Gallahorn...* And she *does* imagine it, the nearness of it all, the happy hexcraft, the togetherness.

Maybe, Aegis thinks, this warped little lass isn't a penalty. A fae trick. Maybe she's supposed to be here.

But as they splash through the tidepools—Aegis pausing to point out periwinkles, brittle stars and urchins, their spikes and arms poking above the low-water's surface—the changeling barks like a seal. Face purpling, teeth lengthening—*teeth! by all the gods it has teeth*—fingernails melding into something wider, harder, *other*, it flails in the loosening blanket, and wails. Aegis sneers. She can't help it. The fae's cry is pitched to shatter fine goblets and harebrained visions. This thing doesn't belong here.

This thing is no one's daughter.

'Hush,' she says, over and over, but without milk or pap, there's no consoling it. Yowls become screeches become manic alarms that are sure to summon trusting folk down from the wharves—fishwives or clamdiggers or anyone with a soul and a breakable heart—for who could ignore such a desperate cry? Not many, she thinks and, one by one, these good Samaritans will abandon their skiffs and stalls to investigate, maybe shouting for the local bailey as they ladder down from the pier only to find Aegis the Cackler alone on the beach with a squalling babe in arms, a child not hers to comfort or carry, and her own sister lately bereft of a newborn—and, oh, what a bind she'll be in then!

There's the first of them now, Aegis thinks. Up on the Flat, Garrup Orr's ambling seawards, the blacksmith moving at a decent clip despite the bulge of his belt and the gout hitching his step. Has he spotted her? Aegis waits a beat, unmoving. No, she thinks. Doesn't seem so. Not yet, anyway. Not yet.

'I'm sorry,' she whispers, laying the wee creature in the nearest tidepool. The cold shocks it quiet, calms it back to humanish form. Soon a squat little girl peers up at Aegis, so innocent she *almost* falters. But then it shrugs and squirms off the blanket. Exposes its unsunned skin to the elements. Smiles and slaps its blue-tinged palms on the water.

Naked and soaked in five-degree weather, it's cozy as a ringed seal on an arctic ice floe.

Rán save us both, Aegis prays, abandoning the changeling to its fate and chases her own into the sea.

OUT AT THE SHILLINGATE ISLES

Some days, Gert tells herself it's the blisters scaring folk away from her stall on Barradoon harbour. The fresh yellow clusters in the crooks of her mouth. The older, darker beads blotching her lips. Her pink-weeping smiles.

Lately, Gert doesn't smile much.

What a sight she makes, chap-cheeked and salt-scoured from working on her Da's rented trawler. The spotlights they rigged to its mast are so much harsher than daylight, glaring on Gert's every flaw. The grease dreading her locks, the crows-feet stamped round her eyes, the calluses and cracks roughing her hands. Her bloody, gods-awful kisser.

Gert nets maybe a quintal of mackerel each night, maybe half that in haddock, but more Devils-own eels than an honest shareman like Abe Mews knows what to do with. Tricksters of the deep, her Da calls them. Snakes so heavy they'll set the wharf scales singing, but those big bodies of theirs are more bone than meat, those fat bellies bloated with poisonous bile. Gert tunes Abe out while he nags, keeps her eyes on the wriggling catch. Huffing and hauling, she fights off scrawking gulls, separates the silvers from the slinkers. Throws nothing back.

Everyone down Gallahorn way knows she's a fool for tricksters.

Always was, always will be. Try as she might to resist them. To side-step them. To undo the wrongs they've already done.

Night after night, Gert tramples more eels than she buckets. Her bare feet squash them on deck like tubes of roe paste, guts and gore spurting, the clear liquid scalding. Within seconds red welts speckle her soles and ankles, right up to the turned cuff of her otter-slick pants. She grits her teeth, grabs a bailer. Sluices away the sting.

No market's black enough to buy *that* deadly spit, Abe Mews insists as she cleans up the lost poison before it can do unwanted damage. He goes to say something else, coughs instead. His thoughts carved like runes in his brow, deep and easily read.

Your fate's not fixed, lass. It's never too late to change.

Tell that to Bear Ingersen, Gert thinks, wishing she could wash off the sting of *him* so easily.

Tell it to Marten.

Tell it to every last one of the Staggs.

As their drifter docks in the blue hour before dawn, she scoops another bucketful of the things. Snuffs the spotlights. Staggers down the gangway, her spine ever more slumped from lugging her bitter hauls up-harbour, home. Alone.

On the farthest-flung arm of Barradoon harbour, Gert's houseboat clunks against a tin and timber pier. Barnacles spackle its hull above the waterline, paint snows from warped weatherboard slats, and the roof's shingled curve is less cheerful than it once was, more frowning. As night fades into morning, Gert unlocks the screen door and slips inside. The air is thick with cloves, lavender, mildew and fish. Everything is in need of a varnish: pine walls, arched ceiling, single bunk, bulkhead. Newspapers are stacked neatly by the sink, gutting knives are sharp inside the chest of drawers, and a collection of tiny glass vials glitters on narrow shelves above the kitchen table. The calico curtains Gert pulls across windows and portholes are moth-eaten but frilled with lace. Her grandmother's brass lamp is polished to gleaming, though it hasn't burnt true since Marten threw a sill-shaped dent into its belly.

I built this boat with my own hands, her once-husband had shouted—forgetting for a moment, as he hurled the lantern so hard its flame guttered out, that this house was *hers* by law and bride price—*and with these hands I'll burn it.*

Later, Marten claimed it was intentional, this misfire. No matter what Gert had done, he'd said, to him, to their marriage, he'd never harm her. And *he'd* never harm a child.

There's no babby, she'd said quietly. Honestly, by then. *Only me.*

You're unbelievable, Marten had said, but not at all like he used to, not in the happy post-tumble whisper she'd loved, that quilt-muffled warmth. *Unbelievable.* That night his voice had glubbed like the oil from her Gran's lamp on the floor. Cold and thin and wet.

I'm no monster, Gertie, he'd said, leaving her to clean up the mess. Leaving her.

Not that *he* needs to be, Gert thinks now, as she spreads newsprint on the floor, fetches a thumb-sized bottle from the shelf, a galvanized tub from the cupboard, and dumps tonight's eels into it. Not with the Stagg women behind him.

Some days Gert blames herself for the uneven trade at her Barradoon market stall. Few can meet her eye anymore, what with the blisters, the wind-chafe, the reek of desperation. But most days, she knows it's *their* fault, not hers.

Those witches she once called in-laws.

No one wants to haggle with a pariah.

Gert snicks the eels' gullets with a tapered blade, bends their spines and hers, then leans in for quick, lip-searing kisses. Three or four deep draws and her mouth is afire, her teeth aching and tongue burnt senseless. Careful not to swallow more than a few drops, she spits poison into the vial. The caustic stuff etches weird patterns into the glass. Soon the bottle's swirling full, the eels safely empty.

At the sink, Gert takes a shot of black screech for gargling and good luck. Spits again, though it still stings, then twists a stopper on the poison before answering the quiet tap-tap-tap on her door.

'It's me, love,' comes a whisper on the other side. The accent's unlike any other Gert's known, syllables stressed in strange places, tone pitched for musical ears. It's a voice fit for mainland mummers, b'ys who paint themselves pretty, lasses who sing like their souls are on fire. 'Open up.'

Even in the dim before dawn, Low-key Highsson gleams like a copper penny. The mismatched buttons on his waistcoat are military brass, crude amber, wish-thin rounds of abalone. The beads threaded through his red locks are a fancy of gemstones and wire. Lamplight on the harbour glints off his boot buckles and bracelets. The distant flames waver in his sly eyes as the houseboat bobs on the tide. He reaches through the gap Gert's cracked in the door, palms the little bottle.

'Not too much,' she says. Same thing every night. Not too much. 'Just enough to—'

'Girl,' Low-key cuts her off. Winks as he does that *thing* with his hands. That butterfly-blur of his fingers. The vial darkens, dullens. Glass becomes air becomes paper and string. She's seen him do it dozens of times now, this trick, but still can't see how he pulls it off. He waggles the teabag like a bell before tucking it into an embroidered vest pocket. 'I got you.'

'I owe you one,' Gert says, blowing a kiss.

Low-key waves it off. Coattails flare as he spins on a chunky heel, lilts off the boat and onto the boardwalk. Water slaps against the planks and pilings, soft as his unearthly tread. 'Hush, you,' he says. 'We're not even close to that yet.'

'You *sure* you aren't still carrying?'

Pippa Stagg furrows her overplucked brows, contemplating Gert's belly. Marten's sister hups the toddler in her arms, shifting little Beetie from one round hip to the other, then turns to her mother for a second opinion.

'Either Gert's apron strings have shrunk in the washtub or she's been opening her—' Pippa pauses, just long enough, dramatic witch that she is, '—*door* to young strangers at night again. What d'you ken, Ma?'

Gert cringes. One mistake, she thinks—and in a flash, Bear Ingersen's there at her houseboat door, his hands are all over her, his seafarer's beard is rasping against her neck, breasts, ribs. Other ticklish parts. One mistake, Gert thinks, shaking the past from her mind. One she'd remedied ages ago, but still, always, she's paying for it.

She lets out a slow breath as battleship Ballantine heaves up to the counter of her fish stall. Heavy of hull and broad of beam, Ma Stagg is in no shape to measure anyone else's kit, but that doesn't stop her. She sneers at Gert's snug smock, dark gaze skimming the rolls around her middle, before pretending to inspect the sleek mackerel Abe had trundled over that morning to supplement Gert's own catch. With snub fingers, Ballantine pinches a fin here, lifts a tail there, tugging fish one by one out of their neat silver rows.

'Old habits die hard,' Ma Stagg says, picking up a lovely lean haddock, turning it this way and that. A fine sheen of oil rainbows across the skin—proof of freshness, Gert knows. Good quality. Ballantine tosses it back onto a packed tray of ice. Makes a show of scrubbing her hands on a scrap of good linen.

'More to the point,' she says to Pippa, scrubbing, scrubbing, as if those very hands hadn't been wrist-deep in cod guts the past forty-odd years, as if they hadn't pawed as many cockles as coins in that time, as if they had ever truly been *clean*, 'if Marten's *ex*-missus is once more *expecting*,' Ballantine's chins wobble as she nods, accepting her daughter's snort of praise, 'then another big change must be on the way, too. Right, Gertie? A new babby calls for a new name, wouldn't you say? Or, better yet, an *old* one.'

Gert crouches to tear a broadsheet off the stack she keeps behind the counter. Her cheeks are still hot as she straightens. Unfolding the paper, she keeps her head down and reaches for the fish Ma Stagg discarded. Gert hears the thick butter in the other woman's lungs and she wants to look up, she wants to confront the bulge of Ballantine's plum pudding eyes, she wants to hold that awful gaze until it narrows, and then, when the old witch starts to wonder what the Christ has got into her, what's put this boldness into meek little Gert Mews, she wants to smirk in just the right way to express, with nothing but a blistered twitch of her mouth, *You're no better than me, hag. Marten knows it. Everyone knows it.*

But too often what folk *know* and what they *believe* are like two halves of an oyster left to rot on the beach. The shell never sits quite true, no matter how hard it's pressed, not once the meat bloats things all out of shape.

And speaking of bloating bellies, Gert wants to say with her slyest Low-key grin, *how's* yours *been faring these days?*

Oh, if only she could see the old witch react to *that*. What she wouldn't give! To watch *her* gaze drop, for once, to see it scrambling over mackerel and haddock and cod, *flick flick flick*ing so fast only Gert would notice, only Gert would understand the desperation in that swift movement, Ballantine's silent, speedy searching of fins and gills, searching, searching, as if, written across those tiny scales, she might find the true meaning behind Gert's words.

How's your *belly faring these days*, Gert would say, and her smile would be hideous but huge because maybe Ma Stagg's innards, which must've been turning for weeks now, her bowels slowly and steadily spoiling, not mortally but queasily so, maybe her innards would choose that very moment to rumble and thunder, and maybe, as she suddenly realised who'd caused that churn in her guts, that it was *Gert* who was smart enough to best her like this, and maybe, as she struggled to figure out how Gert had done it, mousy Gert Mews who hadn't a speck of magic in her, as she racked her nasty brains for the answer, *any* answer, to that question, maybe *then* foul winds would messily *praaaap* from the witch's hind end. And then, maybe, she'd finally understand what it felt like. Being so shamed.

Maybe *then* she'd leave Gert alone.

Now Gert wraps the fish tightly, pretending Ma Stagg is a customer, that she'll fry it up later with shallots and dill, gobble it down with her special tea. She weighs the five-penny parcel in her hand. Considers simply handing it over. *No charge*, she might say, magnanimous. Benevolent conqueror.

But.

'Too right, Ma,' Pippa says. 'High time she fixed her name. After all, any bub of Gert's is a Mews through and through.'

Ballantine nods. '*Any* babby, indeed. This, that, or t'other one. Not a Stagg among them.'

'There's no babby,' Gert says to the fish. On the newspaper

wrapping, there's a half-page ad for an art exhibit that ended over a year ago. Enormous still lives, fish and things dredged from the deeps, piled dead on storm-tossed shores. Done by some painter from the mainland, enchanted, as they all are eventually, by the sea. 'It's just me.'

It was Kelloway's famous black rum that poured Low-key into Gert's life, soon after it almost pummelled him right out of his.

After sinking a half-pint or three at the tavern that night, Gert had slurred her way down to Barradoon harbour, where Abe had caught one whiff of her woeful breath and chose to weigh anchor alone.

Walk it off, lass, he'd said, stowing the nets she usually worked. Locking her oar back in place. No snide remarks. No reprimands. Just quiet understanding. *Tomorrow's a new day.*

So it is, she'd replied, or something like. *See you then.*

After a season of howling rain, the clouds had wrung themselves out. The autumn gales had gentled, gusting sky-tatters away. Timber wharves had turned to cobbles, to grass, to sand, to wildheath trails as Gert blurred her way down the coast. Walking for hours, or so it had seemed, going all over the place, going nowhere. A fortune of stars had jangled in the heavens, their fiery tails swooshing as she wobbled uphill to a viewpoint across from the Shillingate Isles. It wasn't much of a view, nor much of a point, Gert had thought. Just a scuffed patch of rock on the headland, a birdwatcher's bench, and a ragged footpath tripping back down the slope to Kelloway's pub. Right back where she'd started.

Small islands spread like inkblots on the water below, the furthest ones long and low on the glimmering surface, a midnight pod of breaching humpbacks. The closest, though, was what folk stopped to see: a chunk of limestone big as three cathedrals and steepled with ancient pines. At that late hour, the grotto was almost invisible, but Gert fancied she saw its snaggle-toothed maw in the moonlight, sucking and swallowing waves. Spitting nothing back out.

Oh, how she'd shivered then, so hard she fumbled the silver coins from her belt-pouch to palm. One by one, she'd counted them out and tossed them into the brine, a steady gulp of counter-curses drowned by the wind, by the wailing. How many weeks had passed since Bear Ingersen's first starlit knock—Eighteen? No, twenty! As many weeks as she was years old, she'd decided, giving the sea a ha'penny for each. Six since Gert had gone to the drift-spinner's hut to buy a bottle of her most potent corrective. Four since Marten had found the drained jar, the bloodied rags she'd intended to bury. Two since he'd left her. One since the Stagg witches had trashed her fish stall. A few days since she'd first found herself here, cheeks wet and insides churning, tossing pennies at the lonely isles.

All of her happiness had gone into the babby, hadn't it. Bear's own little cub. It had soaked up her joy, or so she'd thought, its tiny body bubbling with her love and laughter. And she'd gone and rinsed it out with Winnifletch's potion, hadn't she just. Mirth and motherhood vanished in one vile-tasting shot, one guts-wrecking day in the privy.

As the moon started its slow downhill roll, Gert had sleeved her face dry—and yet the crying went on. Not hers, she'd realised after a rum-soaked moment. Someone—something?—else's. She'd swerved away from the viewpoint, stared down the footpath. Listened.

Hard to tell if that was whimpering or whinnying.

Gert had staggered after the sound in the silver-blue darkness, chasing it closer to Kelloway's. Hoofs clopped on the cobbles ahead, sparks flashing as horseshoes struck stone. Shadows galloped past the tavern, past *her*. A herd of Gallahorn b'ys on their Da's sleek stallions, a few Orr lads following on skittish ponies. Bellies swilling with at least a keg of the black stuff, they'd hooted and snorted as they fled, lobbing insults like smoke bombs behind them.

'Watch it,' Gert had snapped, or something like, Abe's most vibrant slurs pouring fast from her perfect lips and onto the figure writhing— whimpering? whinnying?—in the gutter.

'Hush,' she'd said softly, reaching down to help, wincing as the poor thing rolled onto its back. What a number those b'ys had done on it. A gaudy mess, she'd thought. Brighter and brasher than Joseph's own dream-coat: purples mashed into a beautiful, angular face; moss-muds ground into slender knees and shapely hind end; ditch-deep reds that drenched shirtfront and trousers, dripping in the crook of its legs. Still some of the ugliest shades Gert has ever seen. The worst colours folk inflict on each other.

'Hush, now,' she'd said. 'Let's sit you up.'

After some wrangling, she'd got him—for it *was* a man after all—upright and, somehow, to his unsteady feet. 'You don't have to do this,' he'd begun, words whistling through the new gaps in his grimace, but *hush*, Gert said again, and that was that. A strange look had crossed his face then, one Gert still can't describe, something between curiosity and calculation, and before she knew it, he'd nodded, draped a cloak-heavy arm across her shoulders. Together they'd taken one step out of the gutter and the next right onto the gangway leading up to her boathouse door.

A wave of vertigo had crashed into Gert as their feet hit the planks. Her head buzzed with transistor static. Impossible to reckon the jump they'd made between *there* and *here* without taking into account the strength of Kelloway's rum, or the mischief in the man's odd grin.

'What are you?' she'd blurted, mishearing the answer through his laughter, the dull hum in her ears. He'd given a name, but it couldn't be right. Not with those trinkets in his wild hair, the layered brocades under his tailcoat, the gems bristling on each of his fingers.

'Low-key?' She'd over-enunciated each syllable, feigning sobriety the way drunks and the incredulous do.

'Close enough,' he'd replied. 'Maybe think of it as a stage name? Purely ironic.'

'Ah,' Gert had said, scraping the key around and around the doorknob, finally connecting with the lock. 'You're a magician, then.'

Oh, how the trickster had laughed.

'Close enough,' he'd said again, following Gert inside. 'Close enough.'

'Is it true what they said? Those Gallahorn b'ys. About the foal?' Gert had bandaged Low-key's cuts and scrapes, dabbed witch hazel onto his bruises, wrapped him in a flannel housecoat. Then they'd sat at her small kitchen table, drinking down other hurts. 'Did a *kelpie* really come out of you?'

Not that it mattered, one way or another. Gert knew all too well that gossip travelled even faster than they had between Kelloway's ditch and her own doorstep. She knew how swiftly its damage was done.

'Girl,' Low-key had said with a sad chuckle. 'You know how it goes when a man's keen to pound some flesh. Any excuse'll do.'

'Hm.' Gert had shifted in her seat, uncorking another tall-neck. Whiskey blurped on the table as she overshot their cups.

'Besides,' Low-key went on, studiously straight-faced. 'It was an eight-legged *horse*, strong and grey, not some flimsy black water-borne spirit. Don't even think for a second I'd shred my nethers birthing anything less.'

Even now, Gert can't recall ever laughing so hard or so long as she had that night. In truth, she doesn't remember much of what they'd said, only the feeling that came with the saying, the bone-deep sense that Low-key understood how it felt to be cast out, always judged by folk with bigger and more ancient family trees, folk whose opinions could empower or impoverish on a whim. Low-key understood it all, Gert knew. He understood *her*.

But then Gert had woken to a house so quiet, she feared he'd been a rum-fuelled dream. A flamboyant figment of her imagination. The chairs had been tucked away, the table cleared and cleaned, and the housecoat he'd borrowed was hooked, as usual, in the closet. Heading down to the harbour as dawn pinked the sea, Gert couldn't decide which was worse: this proof that she was pathetic, a girl her age, alone, glugging and giggling away the dark hours; the humiliation curdling her already sour belly (why *had* she kept drinking? why had she left Abe to trawl the seas without her, again? when had she become such a flake?); or the fact, tried and tested, that her father would've stuck by her, regardless. That night, and always. He'd never leave her stranded.

Sure as sugar, Gert knew she'd find her stall well stocked that morning. Abe would've filled his own first, of course—he loved Gert beyond reason, but he wouldn't bankrupt himself to save her—but he'd never let her open shop without something worthwhile to sell. He wouldn't let her confront the Stagg witches empty-handed.

Except, Gert had thought, doubly cursing herself as she rounded the bay. For a few hours, thanks to Low-key, she'd managed to forget what they'd done to her booth. What *she'd* done to rile Marten's kin. There wasn't much left anymore for Abe to replenish. Not much Ballantine and Pip hadn't already smashed or taken.

Except?

Reaching the site of her shambles on the pier, Gert had stopped. Stared.

'You look queasy as a bagful of eels,' Low-key had said, straightening the bunting he'd just strung on her stall. Seagulls on the yardarm of a nearby sloop watched him with gimlet eyes. All the slurs had been scrubbed from the stall's wooden slats. The saltworn timbers were unhacked and unsplintered. The striped awnings hung untorn. Large ice-trays jutted from the counter on their usual, unbroken angles. Their displays glimmered, richly shoaled.

Low-key had stepped back to admire his handiwork. The early sun still skimmed the sea, but from the tips of his burgundy boots to the bells tinkling in his locks, every inch of Low-key had glowed. Every seam of his tailcoat was perfectly snug, the brocade vests underneath newly sewn. As he uncrossed his arms, Gert had seen clean shirtsleeves, cufflinks. There was dirt on his hands, sure, a smudge of something on his nose, but every tooth had returned to his grin.

'How on earth,' Gert had said, stopping to take it all in. Her stall, somehow just as it used to be, somehow better. And *him*. Standing there calm as the doldrums. Brushing the dust from his palms. All of the night's terrible colours washed off, all those bruises and bashes undone. No bandages. No blood.

Nothing to show what he'd suffered, only what he'd salvaged.

'Magic,' Gert had whispered. 'You *are* a magician.'

'It took a bit of elbow grease, a bit of flair.' He'd tapped his temple with an unscraped finger. Winked. 'A bit of mind over matter.'

Shaking her head, Gert had floated around her market berth. The gulls were quiet as the breeze and the boardwalk barely creaked underfoot while she'd surveyed Low-key's repairs and improvements. He could downplay it all he wanted, but Gert knew real magic when she saw it. Any *bit* of this was more potent than all of Winnifletch's hex-juice combined. A hundred times stronger than any potion Gert had ever guzzled.

Inside, she'd dropped her bag on the floor—not a skewed plank that rocked with each step, but a solid floor! Weatherproofed and tiled with bluestone and slate!—and looked out at the other traders hauling wares along the wharf, propping tarps and tents, slowly unshuttering their stalls. It had suddenly seemed so different, this view she'd glared at for years. All those ships in the harbour, most of them old and grey as the moon, had bobbed gaily on welcoming waters. The beach and bouldered cliffs were less dreary, less drab. The huts strewn like flotsam far up the coast were more like shards of sea glass than sea junk. Even the Shillingate Isles had shone like flecks of mica in the distance, no longer sucking all the light and luck from the area, greedy as bogwater coal.

In that moment, Gert had believed in happiness.

Imagine what else he could do, she'd thought. Low-key was no ordinary driftspinner. No selfish, vindictive witch.

'Oh gods.' Gert said, tasting bile. 'The Staggs are going to *hate* it.'

'And there are those eels again,' Low-key had joked, growing serious when Gert's legs gave out. Quick as fate, he was in the booth and easing her onto a cushioned stool. Leaning forward, she'd folded her arms on the counter. Rested her head.

'Who did this to you?' he'd asked as she shivered and wept. Simple as that. Not *what* did this. *Who.*

Oh yes, Gert had thought. He understood.

Out it had spewed then, the whole sorry tale, like a bucket of chum onto the new stone floor. Of course there were eels in her guts, she'd said, *of course* there were. Marten's kin had put them in there, hadn't they just, she'd been cursed the instant she crossed them. How long ago was that? Weeks? Months? *Feels like years and years now I've been sick*, Gert had said. Sick in love with Marten Stagg, sick with his being off fishing with the b'ys ten months of the year, sick of failing to live up to his family, his name. Sick from the mistake she'd made with Bear Ingersen—the several mistakes, if she's honest, and she was now, she was straight-up with Low-key, with him she wouldn't be anything but. Sick, so sick, from that first squirm in her belly, that first babby she'd never had. So sick after drinking Winnifletch's potion, so sick it's a gods-honest miracle the bub wasn't the only one to lose its life that day.

But then Pippa had come by the houseboat for a cuppa and cake, as she had most mornings, they'd been friends then, or so Gert had thought, not just in-laws but *friends*, and Pip had seen the state Gert was in, mid-purge and full-paining, and maybe Pip had been there herself at some point, maybe she'd suffered such sickness, Jesus Christ and the gods only knew. All the same, Pippa's eyes and heart had hardened that day, as she'd stood outside Gert's privy and added two plus two, reckoning the months her brother had been at sea, the impossibility of this particular sickness being any of his doing.

Oh, how she'd cursed then and so had been cursed; for what Pippa had guessed, Ballantine soon *knew*.

'Those Stagg witches are ruthless,' Gert had said, no lighter for having offloaded. Still, the eels roiled. Still she ached. 'They're *relentless*. Cross them once and you're ruined forever.'

'What they need,' Low-key had said, 'is a swig of their own bitter brew. Let me help. After all, I owe you one.'

'You've already done so much,' Gert had replied. 'I don't know how I'll ever repay you.'

'Just listen,' Low-key had said, 'then tell me what you think.'

So Gert had listened to his plan.

She'd listened.

And thought.

And agreed to it.

Ever since, Low-key has had a way of appearing right when Gert needs him. Like now, as Ballantine Stagg curls a whiskered lip and Pippa steps away from the stall, snugging a faded black shawl around little babby Beetie—as if *Gert* gives her the chills, not the great trays of ice laid out on the counter, nor the grey sea breezes spinning into the bay—and as the fish sogs in Gert's outstretched hand, she hears his reedy whistle jaunting up the pier, and silently thanks all the gods she won't have to face these witches alone today.

'Here you are!' Low-key flutters his hand at the women, pitches his tone somewhere between shock and hurt. He flounces over, bells a-jingle with the force of his huff, but when he reaches Ballantine's side Low-key simpers and slides his arm under her plump elbow, pulling her close as a confidante.

'Didn't we say seven? I saved our table at Ma Clary's, but she's almost out of biscuits already—those Calhoon girls are *insatiable*, aren't they? Pigs at the trough, the lot of them. Just about made me gag, watching the hogs eat.'

'We weren't more than two minutes behind you, right Pip?' Ma Stagg says with a titter. A titter! Gert has to look away or else she'll laugh in the hag's withered face, she'll laugh until she cries, and ruin everything.

Ignore what I say when they're around, Low-key had told her. *Better yet, ignore* me.

What an actor, Gert thinks, stealing glances as Low-key flits and flaps over the Staggs. Gossiping like he's known them all his life, rather than a handful of months. She finds a cloth and wipes down her knives while Low-key out-snarks and out-snipes the spellbound women, steering them away from Gert's stall without so much as a howdy-do. As they retrace his steps down the pier, Low-key's voice trails after them like strong cologne, heady and offensive. They *would* sting, the barbs he's throwing now—how fine ladies like Pip and Bal shouldn't associate with fishwives like Gert, the stink of wharf trash sticks like a burr, and so on—it *would* if she didn't know better. If she wasn't in on the trick.

What an actor, she thinks again with a small twist in her belly. Excitement. Nerves. Doubt? Gert pauses. No, she thinks, turning to serve one of the Rideout lads, passing him half a pail of stripped eels for bait, adding three pennies to his tab. She can't doubt Low-key now. Not after he's gone this far, done this much. Every second day for months, he's broken his fast with the witches. He's watched them shovel biscuits and butter into their gobs, smiled at their stories, served up tea with his gossip. Every second day, he's replaced Ma Clary's ancient teabags with the ones Gert prepared. The ones *they* made, the two of them, together. Every second day, he's steeped the brew perfectly. Never long enough to kill, never short enough to waste time or poison. Just enough to upset their horrible guts.

Just enough to hurt.

It's going to work, she thinks, no ifs, ands, or buts. It's got to work.

A few regulars keep Gert in business for another day. It's the same most mornings, the tide of cash always washes in after Ballantine has unmoored from Gert's stall, carried by folk brave or foolish enough to risk buying from a blistered *ex*-Stagg. Their custom fills more than her purse.

It's something, Gert thinks as she closes up around noon and heads home for a snooze. It's better than nothing.

That night, after hauling more than her share of mackerel onto Abe's trawler, twice that much haddock, and a ten-minute-nag's worth of eels; after ignoring her Da, again, as always, and sloshing two bucketfuls of the tea-makers onto her houseboat; after slicing and sucking and spitting out the vile stuff; after a bunch of new blisters are barnacling her lips and two new phials are sparkling with poison, Gert has nothing else to do but wait for Low-key's *tap-tap-tap* on her door.

She waits.

And waits.

And waits.

And then, she worries.

Brass bells summon worshippers to churches and groves the next morning. Crick-necked and bleary from dozing all night at the table, Gert ups-awning on her fish stall and watches ant-lines of folk marching mindlessly off to their prayers. She doesn't expect to find Low-key among their numbers—he doesn't strike her as a godly man—and yet she hopes to see flashes of copper and burgundy amid the pious black. She hopes to hear trills of tooth-whistling between steepled gongs. She hopes he's still hearty, still hale, still *here*.

She's not ready to add him to the list of men who've left her.

She simply won't accept that he's gone.

Hours drag, slow and heavy as Abe's nets in high summer, despite the hustling trade on the wharf, the banter and barter between merchants and men. Gert's own trays are cleaned out long before the lunch-tide, before even the Stagg witches have swooped on her stall. But on a day devoted to blessings, Gert's in no mood to count her own. Not with this tattle of bottles in her apron pocket, their poison uncollected, unconverted, unconsumed. Not without Low-key here grinning and gabbing and doing that *thing* with his hands, reshaping everything as it should be, making it all somehow okay.

Another night on the water, another blistering bucketful caught and cut against her Da's wishes, another two vials filled and carefully capped. Then another wake-up kink in Gert's neck, another sinking chill in her belly, another dawn blooming red without Low-key's polished nails tap-tapping on her door. Once more she sets off to Barradoon harbour with a pocketful of poison. No teabags. No new favours owed. No promises waved off with a humble, *Not yet.*

No sign, here or there, of Low-key.

'I don't get it,' Gert mutters, slumped on the padded stool he'd given her, searching her stall's perfect tiles for answers. Playing peekaboo with the clouds, the sun is relentlessly bright for late autumn and so warm even the soft southern traders have shed their winter-sea coats. In shirtsleeves and apron, Gert shivers despite the heat. Something isn't right, she's *sure* of it. Something's gone terribly wrong. Low-key isn't like Bear or Marten or the rest of the local b'ys. He wouldn't have up and sailed without telling her. Without saying goodbye.

Maybe it's a new trick, Gert tries to convince herself. Some new twist in their plan, some new angle he must've explained when she was only half-listening. Something that would keep him occupied—and away—for a couple of days. Him *and* the Stagg witches. Something only he could do, with a wink and a wave of his magic hands. Something in a secret elsewhere.

'What are you up to?' Gert wonders aloud.

'It's ointment,' Abe Mews says. Gert sits up with a start; it's not like her Da to come round so late in the morning. She hadn't registered the familiar shuffle of his boots on the pier, the pipeweed rumble deep in his chest. Now he clears his throat, fiddling with an old pomade tin before placing it on the counter. 'For your mouth,' he explains and pops the lid, revealing an oval of oyster-hued goop. 'Winnifletch says it's no cure-all, but it's got lavender or somesuch in there.' He shakes his grey head, embarrassed. 'You know, herbs and stuff. Supposed to be soothing.'

'Oh, Da,' Gert says, dabbing some on before giving him a small, slightly eased smile. Always the mother hen, she thinks, not unkindly. No matter whose babby she's lost, no matter whose kin she's offended, no matter how ugly she's got these past few months. Old Abe always looks after her.

Maybe that's why she asks, 'You seen Pippa lately?'

Something in Gert's voice makes her Da pause before answering. The gullish airiness, perhaps. The subtle cracks. Or maybe it's just that she's asking after Pip Stagg at all, after downing so many drams to forget her.

'Don't think so,' he says at last. 'But she's tight with those Gallahorn b'ys, isn't she? Might want to give them a yell.'

The last thing Gert wants is to talk to *those* louts, but short of calling in at the grand house on Hopewell Square, something she hasn't done since Marten last weighed anchor, something she's got no intention of ever doing again, Gert can't see how else she'll track down Low-key. All this time, he's only ever come to her, never the other way around. Oh, she's been dying to see his place; the overflowing jewellery chests she imagines he's got, the closets bursting with rainbows. She pictures a property far away from the harbour; a snug cabin nestled on actual land. No creaky houseboat for him. No wandering address, changing from wave to wave. Knowing him, there'll be a pretty pond to reflect the full moon, a vegetable patch roiling with pumpkins, a birch grove filled with songbirds. A deep wishing well. A little stable for his eight-legged horse-babby.

Trudging the path to Kelloway's, Gert snorts at the thought of Low-key mucking shit like a farmhand. But as she pushes through the tavern's heavy door, her mirth gets smothered in the fug of body heat, smoke, and ale-breath stewing in the low-beamed room. A single sweep of Gert's tired eyes confirms what her heart's been growling the whole way here: right about now, there's none but the desperate and the three o'clock drunks seeking truths in Kelloway's pint glasses.

Gert slides into a booth at the back, signals for a cup of the black stuff. Before she's shouldered out of her jacket, the barkeep clunks two tumblers onto the narrow table. 'Second one's on me,' he says in his comforting, oak-barrel voice. 'Looks like you need it.'

'Thanks,' she says, sinking both shots, thinking the extra one won't hurt. Better to numb the worry before it gnaws her ragged. For a while, her head whips up each time the door opens, fresh air gusting in with folk she isn't here to find. *Something's wrong.* She toys with the empty glasses, then raises two fingers at the bar. Gives Kelloway a few silvers to cover the last round, a few more for this one. Drinks everything but the dregs. *No Gallahorn b'ys, no Stagg witches, no Low-key.* Hinges squeak, greetings are laughed or clapped or bellowed. Late afternoon exhales into early evening. *There is no new plan, no trick I've missed. There's only the old one.* Soon all the barstools are taken, windblown latecomers wedging in to order drinks. *Maybe he's overdosed them. Pip and Ballantine. Maybe they're dead and rotting in a shallow grave somewhere, eyes wide and tongues blue, Ma Clary's breakfast biscuits a-sludge in their bellies, poison-tea glossing their lips.* Quick-drinkers huddle around the wine casks Kelloway's stood on end here and there, their red fists slamming back as much froth as it takes to stave off the night's lonesome dark. *Maybe he's hightailed it out of here before anyone finds out he killed them.* Gert sways to her feet, flaps for a refill. *Before anyone learns it was actually me.*

Change clanks against the ointment tin in her pouch. She smears on a thumbful while Kelloway dips into the sack and counts out his due, not a cent more. He gives the table a quick wipe, then he's gone. *Hurting to help.* Gert smudges her greasy mouth on a pint glass. *Isn't that the old saying?* She gulps around the lump in her throat. *He's hurting to help me.*

But that seems backwards to her, somehow.

This time, after the door screeks open, Gert finds herself outside. The pub's warmth behind her, a light mist damping her face. *Walk it off, girl,* Gert's Da says, good old Abe always looking out for her, no matter how much she disappoints. *Walk it off.* Shivering without her jacket, she hugs her purse close and takes his advice.

Lanterns bob overhead, they clang on a windowsill, *I built this boat with my own hands,* they glow too close and too hot, *and with these hands I'll burn it,* they gutter between strides, pale orbs staggering, cooling, sailing up with the silvering moon. Gert trips past the ditch where the Gallahorn b'ys first pounded Low-key into her life; it's empty tonight, only a trickle of water through the meadowsweet, footprints trampled in the mud. No kelpies. No horses. No pretty men.

Up on the Shillingate viewpoint, she parks herself on the bench and dredges her pouch for wishes. Counter-curses. Shining circles of luck. Over and over, her blunt nails clang against metal. Her fingers jellyfish inside the leather bag, clanging and clanging, but the coins keep eluding her, they're stuck behind this stupid tin; no, they're all glimmering across the cloudless sky; no, they're already plink-sinking deep into the simmering sea.

No, they're all in *there,* Gert thinks as she tilts forward into the wind and squints out at the Shillingate Isles. The headland crashes against her knees and now her palms are stinging, lumped with gravel. She crawls closer to the cliff's rugged edge, sits like a picture book sphinx, and waits for the ground to slow its spinning. After a while, the horizon settles and Gert can focus without wanting to puke.

There they are, she thinks, peering across the water at the largest island.

Light glitters in the grotto at its base. Not just moon-silver, but something else, something gold, something copper, something red. A dragon's hoard of coins washed up on the cavern's rocks. Tiny flames of hope, Gert thinks, all her wishes beckoning. Flickering for her alone.

It takes months for Gert to chase those flicker-flashes down from the viewpoint, years to stumble to Abe's berth on the harbour, a lifetime for his trawler to dock.

'Go back,' she slurs as his hull scrapes along the pier. On the mast, the spotlights are snuffed; there's only an old moon above, an older lamp pegged to the prow, and Abe's oldest instincts to guide the boat home. Now Gert's gripping the sea-slick gunwale, yanking the boat steadier. 'Put about,' she yells as her Da shoulders out of the wheelhouse to see what's shuddered his mooring. Left then right, Gert slings her rum-sodden legs over the plank, skids, and falls to her knees on the scale-speckled deck. Blubbering, she fumbles for an oar. Clunks it overboard. Starts to shove off.

'He's out there, Da. All alone.'

A sigh, no more, and Abe returns to the helm. He gets a hiccupped heading from Gert and lays a course for the Shillingate Isles. A williwaw picks up as they sail, a brutal north wind that keeps Abe's hands glued the spokes, but doesn't stop his jaw flapping free. His ears open.

'Who's this *he*, then?' he asks once the ox-prowed trawler is blustering through the chop, tackling mile after sea-mile with blunt force. The moon's scythe pursues them, sharp and swift, ploughing the waves, a delicate ship-scooping net. 'Who's he to you?'

'A friend,' Gert begins, but Low-key's more than that by now, isn't he. Much more. Not a lover—no, *no*, they'd never, she'd never, *he*'d never, *oh no*—she giggles a bit, but then blubs again soon enough. After Marten, after Bear, all those nameless others, Gert's had a crawful of lovers. With Low-key, she doesn't have to try so hard. She doesn't have to perform. She doesn't have to *please*. All she's ever had to do with him is be. Just *be*.

How can she explain their bond? Forged out of a handful of confidences and one night's soul-sung confessions, this connection only grows stronger with each early morning call, each hurried wharfside chitchat. Starlight trickles down her cheeks as she tries to capture what Low-key has meant to her. What he *means*.

She can't.

Whatever this is, whatever they've got, it's not for other folk's knowing or caring. It's theirs alone. It's *hers*.

'He's someone worth saving,' Gert says at last, spilling what details she can, what troubles Abe might understand. How she and Low-key met. When. Why. The Stagg witches. The eels. The trickster's tea. Their perfect, poisonous plan.

'Oh, Gertie,' Abe mutters. 'Gertie, my girl. You've met your match.'

Meaning the Staggs, Gert thinks blearily, then changes her mind. No, not them. *Him*.

Rounding the cape down Gallahorn way, the boat sheds its ox-skin, becomes a fat walrus galumphing along the coast. We'll never make it,

Gert thinks, bending over the forward keel like a snarling prow-beast, as if she could power them on by sheer will, by shivering weight.

Please, Gert begs the rearing white waves. Please, she demands of the sky's felt-lined coffer, its lid thrown open and jewels twinkling. Please let it not be too late.

Shrieks wilden the headwind as the largest Shillingate isle appears across from the bluffs. Sea-carved and lit from inside, it looms, menacing on the horizon; a giant's candle-gourd discarded, darkly blazing. High, primal sounds yawp from its low, fire-bright grotto.

'Hurry,' Gert whispers, every bit of her straining to reach that under-isle chamber. '*Hurry.*'

Abe steers into the shoreward channel and drops anchor within sight of the grotto. He steadies the rope ladder as Gert climbs overboard, then follows her into the sea. They swim fast to outpace the insidious chill, heads above the star-spangled water, every muscle tense, aching for warmth. By day, the distance between Abe's boat and the cavern mouth isn't far, a fly-fisherman's laziest cast at best, but that night it leaves them both quaking.

The current is calm, the tide retreating. Gert lets the waves push her where they will—she needs their strength and direction—and soon they've washed her up on the sloping stone floor. Catching her breath, she scrapes herself upright. She takes a step, another, until she's all the way inside.

The grotto *is* rich, richer than anything she's ever seen. Everywhere, coins have melded into the ancient limestone. Pennies she herself might've thrown from the headland, plus dollars and sovereigns and time-worn doubloons, each round and thin as church wafers, all gild the cavern's walls. Pirate *reales* and pieces-of-eight have starfished around stalagmites and blunt-topped dripstones. Silver dirhams, with their nice Elvish scripts eroded near-smooth, are clustered like mussels on the uneven, sea-slurping floor. Verdigris rivulets trickle from bits of bronze embedded into the high-vaulted ceiling. It's enchanting; the chamber's strange acoustics, its ethereal shine, the great stalactite hanging dead-centre like some otherworldly chandelier. For a second, Gert stands there dazzled. Relieved. Overjoyed.

Right there, lying directly below that monstrous stone fang, is Low-key.

Oh, how she smiles then, just for a second, a huge lip-splitting smile. 'Thank god,' Gert says, but he doesn't answer, not with words. Low-key can't turn his head, can't see anything but the turquoise bead welling on the fang's hollowed tip, fat and heavy, then dripping onto his upturned face. His stone-bound, scalded, screaming face.

'How did this happen?' Gert cries, scrambling over pebbles and shale to the hideous slab where Low-key lies trapped.

'Who did this?' she asks stupidly, needlessly, while Low-key thrashes and yelps, and the stalactite rains a slow death onto his head.

'We were so careful,' she quavers, staring down at him as her mind flails. 'How did they catch you?'

'You'll get no sense from him now,' Abe says as another drop falls, 'or not yet anyway. Keep him company, lass. Distract him if you can. I'll be back in a minute—stay with him. Stay close.'

Gert nods blankly. She's not going anywhere. It's her fault Low-key's here, isn't it just. The poison, the plan, it was her troubles that started it, her fault. *She* should be lying there, not him. 'Oh, Low-key.'

Another droplet falls. Another scream as it hits.

'Hush,' she clucks to fill the sudden quiet between drips. She reaches out to touch his pale cheek, but hesitates. Afraid she'll hurt more than help. 'Hush, hush.'

Even now, marred and scarred and half-hidden in rock, Low-key is beautiful. His long copper tresses ripple like kelp in the wash, his favourite hair-baubles gleaming. Where the witches have shackled him— fetters hewn of magic and metal and the grotto's own limestone—Low-key's body seems to disappear. His neck and chest, wrists, waist, and ankles are fused into the stone table, the bindings limned with silver and gold shrapnel, radiant with the Staggs' incredible power.

'Take this.' Abe slops up beside her, soaked and shivering after hound-paddling out to the boat and back. He passes Gert an empty worm bucket, keeps the angler's priest for himself. 'Put the poor man out of his misery.'

Blessed silence, for an instant, as Gert holds the pail under the fang's flow.

Then comes the poison's constant, maddening, tin-plinking rhythm.

The wooden crack of Abe's mallet on impervious stone.

Low-key's shuddering breaths.

'You're safe now,' Gert says. 'Tell me what happened.'

Oh, how Low-key writhes, recounting his failure—*their* failure—in duping the Stagg witches. As much as the poison, Gert thinks, this confession pains him. That he, Low-key Highsson, had been outwitted. Outfoxed. Outmatched.

'I should've heard the warnings.' He can only twitch his head in shame. 'Magic always speaks to magic. There's no way of shutting it up.'

'But how—' Gert frowns and closes her mouth. No need to torture him for details. The Staggs had guessed what she'd had in mind; that much is clear. They must've known all along who Low-key is, *what* he is. To Gert. And to *them*.

These witches are harridans, not fools. They have more power than anyone. Always have, always will. And Gert had eeled herself ugly for nothing.

In fact, she thinks, flinching from the fang's mordant *drip-drip*. Maybe this is her very own poison now sizzling into the bucket, eating through the thin metal. Or maybe it's the Staggs' unique brew, conjured in vengeance, carried in secret to the Shillingate isles. Maybe Pip had persuaded the Gallahorn b'ys to ferry it over here. Maybe Ballantine had goaded her wayfaring sons into action. Maybe, Gert thinks, Marten had personally jury-rigged this terrible stalactite for his mother. Maybe he'd filled it, somehow, with Ballantine's worst bile. Maybe he'd held Low-key down while the witches encased him in stone. And maybe, finally, he'd call it even between them.

I'm no monster, Gertie.

Maybe now he'd call the hags off.

'It's no use,' Low-key says. 'If I can't uncast their bindings myself—and, trust me, I can't—no charmless mortal is going to help.'

Still, Abe tries. All that night, he tries. Hammering the fish-bat against coins and coral chains, chiselling ha'pennies and handcuffs, smashing silver dollars and stubborn rock. At last, when the hardwood mallet splinters, then cracks, then splits like a cornhusk in his bleeding hands, Gert's Da changes tack.

'Stay put,' he says, throwing the useless tool, and himself, into the sun-dappled sea. 'Don't give up.'

'Hurry,' Gert says as Abe swims for supplies. Dry clothes. Food. Fresh water. A stronger vessel for all the poison. 'And hurry back.'

Concentrate, Gert reminds herself, again.

After a week in this brilliant, gods-awful place, her own skin has been scalded many times over. Her fingers, hands, and forearms are clad in gloves made of pure poison, pure pain. Holding a dish aloft all this time, protecting Low-key from the witches' abuse—or trying to, anyway, trying her best—Gert has borne the brunt of the Stagg-gall spatter as it steadily *plink-plink-plink*s down from above.

Hurting to help.

Concentrate.

On that first night, Low-key had still had the energy to conjure small flames. For hours, their tongues licked the salt air above his bound hands, their dim light reflected back tenfold on the cavern's coin-laid stone. Back then he'd still had the will for such things. He'd had the gumption to scream.

Nowadays, only the wishiest grey light seeps into the cavern with the tides and near-winter mists. Nowadays, Low-key mostly sleeps.

Mostly in fifteen-minute snatches.

It takes about twenty minutes for the dish Gert's clasping to brim and overflow. It's a porcelain heirloom, big enough to bathe a baby in— Gert herself once splashed in its toll-painted depths, her newborn head and neck cradled oh-so-gently in Abe's tentative, new Dadda hands— and she balances it across both her forearms, carefully grips its scalloped rim, her elbows jammed into her sides to buttress its awful weight. Such a delicate piece, and so heavy. So hard to support.

Concentrate.

Bracing the bowl against her belly, she turns oh-so-slightly. Risks a glance down at the frigate-shaped platform below. Low-key's prison.

Her bare feet straddle his rock-shrouded torso, her legs locked against any rogue waves. She's long abandoned any fear that the Staggs will return to check on him. On her. Those witches are cunning, Gert knows, now more than ever. They've snagged two fish with one hook. They've got us both where they want us.

Already, again, the dish is filling.

Gert blinks and blinks to clear the hex-haze from her vision. Her arms ache, oh how they *ache*. But she can't afford to change position yet, to rub her eyes.

He can't afford it.

Concentrate.

Fifteen minutes makes the most manageable basinful. By then it's about two-thirds full: a dreadful, bearable load. There's much less spillage if Gert breaks her vigil at that point, less slosh and slop as she lowers herself into the ankle-deep swirl of seawater, quickly but cautiously, one aching inch at a time. Always holding the dish above Low-key's ruined face, under the punishment forever falling from above. Their punishment. *Hers.* She does all she can to keep it from landing. Protecting him up to the fifteenth minute, then pulling away for a few seconds, only a few, but far too many.

You don't have to do this, he'd said, when and while he still could.

Don't move, she'd replied, breath fogging as she climbed down and carefully poured the bowl's contents over his fetters, cuffs, collar. Wisps of smoke rose like hope from the bindings, but the poison scarcely left a mark on the stone. No matter how much she collected. No matter how much she continues to spill.

Night and day. Day and night. Up, down. Fill, pour.

It makes no difference.

Concentrate.

If she lets the sea's sough-and sigh lull her, if the fang's rhythmic plinking distracts her, if she stops counting every second and every heartbeat, if she waits even a daydream too long before tipping the shallow bowl, well, Gert Mews isn't the only one who pays for her mistake. Her selfishness. Her weakness.

Again, she thinks. As always.

Night and day.

Day and night.

Low-key barely whimpers now when Gert shifts from her post, the blue-green drops scorching skin but not shackles. She knows the poison's defeating him, burning his magic right out. She scales the rock once more. Waits for the basin to refill.

Up, down.

Fill, pour.

Low-key mutters through his nightmares, weird words Gert can't quite hear, spells that don't translate and don't work. Not yet, Gert believes. Not *yet*.

Concentrate.

More and more, the trickster sleeps.

Night and day.

Day and night.

But.

'Next time Abe comes,' Low-key says between dishfuls, between drowses, 'listen to him. Let him take you home. You don't need to do this, love.'

'Hush, you,' Gert says, trembling but true. Holding the bowl out. Holding on. *Concentrate.* 'I'm not going anywhere.'

Twelve minutes pass, then: 'I owe you one,' Low-key says.

'Hush.' Gert presses her smooth lips together, gets ready to move. Quick. Quick. Down, up. She won't let him suffer. She won't leave him to fend for himself. 'We're not even close to that yet.'

A TANGLESMITHED TALE

There's an old bench on the storm-scrubbed viewpoint o'erlooking the Shillingate Isles, a handmade thing riveted into the clifftop, all scavenged ship-oak and rusted wrought iron. It's not much to look at: solid, functional, as timeless and worn-out as love. Bøda's hounds water its legs once, sometimes twice a day. Arney stumps around with his loopy ears dragging, Cú's blunt muzzle ruffles the scrag-grass, the dainty feet, the palms and pert rumps of bitches who somehow always make it up here before them. Bøda herself isn't one for sitting and knitting, though the Isles are pure magic at dusk—the merrish fins and flukes shearing around those stone titans are a precious sight to behold—and the pew's more than wide enough to accommodate her broad beam. Its weathered planks easily seat two or three weary walkers at once, two or three narrow-eyed gapers, two or three harridans with nothing better to do than pester lone women like Bøda, to spy and sneer and scoff while she stands at the waterside, unravelling.

It's a short enough hike to the lookout from Kelloway's tavern, along a pebbled path Bøda's trudged maybe a hundred times since Davvy turned tail on her, but no less punishing on the knees for all that. She pauses every few steps, huffing like a walrus, sucking life into her lungs. From a pouch at her belt, she tosses the pups chunks of dried herring, saving the sour apples for later. Cú's a real greedy-guts; if Bøda doesn't withhold a treat or two, poor Arney won't get a skerrick. They yip ahead as she resumes the climb. Salt winds rasp her round cheeks, pinking her nose and bare hands; she's bright as a berry long before she reaches the plateau. When at last she does, Bøda turns beetroot.

Shamless mutts.

Cú's flirting with Jezzie and May Calhoon, nuzzling the twins' stickish thighs, hopping to lick their tittering faces. At the bench's far end, Arney's plunked his double chin on the Stagg lass's pretty knee, his big black-coffee eyes glistening, putting on his saddest starveling waif pout.

Little traitors.

'Evening, Bød,' says May, cutting her name short out of spite, making it sound ghoulish. *Booooood.*

'Nice night for netting,' says Jezzie, tone devilish light. 'Think those flimsy rods of yers'll catch any keepers?'

Deep breath in. Bøda shunts her netful of wool from one meaty fist to the other, the makeshift sack bristling with long whalebone needles. She turns away, *slow exhale*, and watches the sun snag its fat belly on the sea's jagged tips, slowly sinking in a crimson dazzle.

'C'mon, Arn,' she says. Quick slap on her thigh before she keeps walking. 'C'mere, Cú,' a single click of her tongue—they don't need telling twice—then it's o'er the rocky brink Bøda goes. No ropes, no harness. Just grit and a prayer to Njörðr and Rán, then a kind thought for Sedna—a great giant of a lass like herself—forever roaming the deeps with her incredible, enchanted fingers. The only guides Bøda even half trusts.

Above and behind her now, the bitches giggle and goss.

To th'abyss with them.

Those stringy-limbed fisherwives won't ever be *her* chosen crew. Wives who only briefly lend their b'ys to the sea, season by season, before reeling them back to hearth and home. Wives spoiled with plump bubs who laugh as they thrive, as they sing, as they eventually, happily, sail off on their own. Wives who park their bony arses up there on the headland, day after day, night after night, nattering as they tat pretty doilies for their tables, needle-hooks far slower and far straighter than their spiteful tongues. Wives who lean *this close* to the precipice Bøda herself o'erleaps on the regular, snooping with pinched brows at the goings-on below. Never trekking down there themselves. Just peeping. Idly condescending.

To th'abyss with them all, Bøda thinks again, cursing those cackling, crowish wives, damning their frivolous hearts and slender ankles and joyfully overfull houses.

The downward trail is spindle-thin, an erratic zigzag carved into the crag by generations of egg-gleaners, squid-jiggers, and folk keen to visit their seal-kin by the breakwater. The way's treacherous even for such nimble men; Bøda herself takes it slow and steady, side-on, while the dogs lollop along like springtime lambs, no fear, no worries, no brains in their blithe little heads. Her mouth quirks. *Pair of fools.* They're yapping at the rush and hush of the rising tide when at last her felted soles touch the seawall's limestone surface. Heat's gushing under the cables of her thick woollen gansey, wicking into her pits and blunt collar, slicking her skin. Once pale as fresh cream, Bøda's sweater is now brown as old porridge, the carefully crafted yarn grimed from her many cliffside clamberings. She wipes her hands down her front, murking the knitted ribs and bobbles. These days, the unique pattern's part dust, part clay, part sweat, part blood. Looks woeful, really, but it's hers. Muss and all.

'Put a plug in it,' she snipes at the dogs, lobbing a ragged hunk of fish to fill Cú's gob with something other than noise for a minute. Arney pads up beside her, noses for a snack. She slips him a scarred palmful of fruit, scritches under his collar, then flings an offering into the water. Waits for cold fingers to snatch the wee apples, waits while they bob beside moorings that haven't housed any boats since Barradoon built a proper harbour. She waits.

It's still a great spot for whiling, Bøda thinks.

Maybe nine cubits across, the seawall is sturdy, stalwart, *steadfast*. From rim to reef, it's glistening with salt and spirit, etched with runes carved by will and wave and wind. Oh, sometimes she fancies it's a medieval rampart, capstoned and crenellated, protecting these fair isles from dragons and oath-breaking knights. But then one of the pups'll skid down its rough seaward slope, claws skittering like dry leaves on the stone, and shatter that image. Then, she'll see a huge drunken wyrm, a proud beast brought low after too many shots of Kelloway's blackest screech, a big old lug spewing foam along the sandy banks. Either way, it's the best place Bøda's found for thinking, knitting, collecting herself.

Holding herself together.

Soon enough winter's aurora will dance o'erhead, veils shimmering in shades of delight, tinting the wool on her needles an unearthly, liquid green. But now, autumn's first stars have just pierced the gloaming, small and sharp and corpse-blue. Bøda snaps, once, and the hounds retreat to the cliff's foot. *Good boy*, she says with another snick of apple for Arn. *Good girl* with a chewy husk of cod for Cú. *Be good*, she prays at the water.

Hers is a vigil of pacing, pondering, planning. As she walks, Bøda grates the pads of her fingers along the wall's runemarks, each angular stroke brimming with solutions. Sparks. Spells. Between steps, Bøda wonders how—*if*—she might call on them again. If her need is sufficient. If they'll answer. Cautiously, she casts her mind wide. Scans the distant shoreline and, much closer, the chop splashing her boots. The sea's star-sprinkled surface swells more than sighs now. Moon-crested waves gnaw the wall's hem, its waist, its barnacled collar. Kelp and blackweed ripple below. Minnows dart around the ticker-tape fronds, silver scales winking in the Shillingates' shadows. The strewn apple-votives float off, untouched. Unworthy. Unwanted.

Left on their own, Arney and Cú start to whimper, antsy, eager for company. Again, Bødo snaps them instantly silent. *Good dogs*, she says with the last of the chew. If only the same trick worked on people.

Far above on the lookout, the pitchy crows cackle.

'Any bites?' one of them yells—probably the Stagg wench, she just can't help herself—and Bøda rolls her eyes. *That's original*.

When she's not alone—which is how it's always been, really, even with Davvy around, even with the furry terrors forever nipping her heels —Bøda gravitates towards *other* company. Childless hens, divorcées, the unattractively single. Women who can't be squeezed into wifely, motherly moulds: they're too big, too small, too much, though they try and try and *try* to fit. Women who exist around the holes in their lives, often filling them, as Bøda does, with good long yarns. These women share her passion for knitting true tales—they're not petty tatterers like the Calhoons and Staggs, but *devoted* woolwenders, *dedicated* tanglesmiths, women so smitten with the knots and plot purls in Bøda's narrative ganseys that they see her superior skills first, her awful size later. Women who actually, openly, *admire* her.

Better than anyone who's worried and whiled on this wall, Bøda can capture a man's life story in one sweater, crafting a pattern that's his and his alone, a pattern so perfect, so individual, that if he should go o'erboard in the thing, if he should drown wearing it, the yarn would still be legible long after the mermaids nibbled every feature from his face. His history will still be there, soaked in its strands, wound in its stitches, trapped in its seams. No one but its knitter can change *that*.

And Bøda's the best tanglesmith in the business.

Will you look at my work, these other women ask her, these broken women, these eager apprentices. *Before you head off on your lonesome*, they say—one or another of them's always awaiting her at Kelloway's, a kind word on their lips and a nightcap on the table—*stay awhile*, they say, balm to Bøda's sorry soul, *stay and tell me how to fix this*.

Please, they say, *tell me what to do*.

And she does. Oh, Bøda knows how to act around *these* women, knows just what to say, what they want to hear—though none of them ever really gets her advice. She tells it like it is, shows what she's done, how she does it, and still. Even so. None of these women can see their flaws, even when she highlights them, over and over. None have Bøda's natural talent for binding. None have her practice. Her purpose. Her patience.

Hours, she'd waited *hours* for Davvy to come home that last night, hours upon hours after months upon months after years upon years of *waiting*. For him to haul in that fortune-filled catch he always swore was just o'er the horizon. For him to finish thatching the byre so's the beasts would quit shivering themselves milkless each winter. For him to put her name on the deed of his house, *their* house these past seven years, to make things official and lawful and permanent. For him to clink the right number of coins into her purse on payday. For him to thank her for the chowder she boiled up special on his birthday, for the clean sheets and coveralls and jocks she pressed every day, for the swept floors and scrubbed chamber pots, for the lunches of rollmops and rarebit and canteens sloshing with cider, for the stocked pantry and larder and root cellar, for the one-of-a-kind Davvy Keen gansey she was knitting *that very moment* on her finest whalebone needles. For him to give her a ring and a crown of flowers, a feast and a pearl-dotted frock, even though she's always pretended marriage doesn't matter; it's the partnership that counts, not the party, or so she's always told nosy folk with their nosy questions. For him to stop lingering later and later at the docks after scouring the puncheon tubs, to stop fraternising, to stop *roving* before dragging his feet back o'er their threshold at dawn. For him to notice the hounds—the little lovesick fools just *adore* him—and credit how well she's trained them. For him to share her bed every night, as he used to, once upon a time, when they were younger and fitter and courting. For him to say he still liked the look of her on his arm, that the extra pounds didn't matter, that he still *wanted* her, *needed* her, that there was simply more of her to love now. For him to be a husband in truth, not in jest. For him to fill her up, heart and body and soul. To cure her bone-deep loneliness.

She'd waited and waited and waited.

Until, late that very last night, she'd had a crawful of lying there on her tossed-and-turned pallet, feigning sleep, waiting for the front door to creak on hinges Davvy'd never got round to oiling, waiting to pounce, waiting to knuckle her weepy eyes and guilt-trip him from here to Gallahorn and back; she was *sick of it*. The waiting. The pretending. The lies.

Quickest way to catch a man's notice is to disappear, Bøda knew. She'd done it before, hared off without a word, taking heirlooms Davvy'd miss once he sobered enough to see straight, taking the dogs, taking her needles and tanglework, taking her own sweet time coming back. Only with her absence and his hangover and no breakfast on to soothe him in the morning, only *then* came regret, apologies and promises, soft looks and soft touches, and at least a good week of making up again. As always, still, Bøda was banking on it.

So. While Davvy was reeling home from the tavern that endless century of nights ago, she threw his favourite blanket on o'er her nightdress, its grey flannel burred from use and shaggy with long strands of his sluffed blond hair, she pinned it on like a cloak with Mither Keen's gold trefoil brooch, snatched up her coin purse and knitting, called for the pups, and left him. Again.

Off she went to the Shillingate viewpoint, where the dogs marked the bench before scurrying down the seaward path. Bøda followed their lead, keen to avoid any and all of Kelloway's revellers. The tavern shone like a chest full of copper, jigs and reels rollicking uphill whenever the heavy door swung open, fiddles and throats screeching glad songs. Maybe it wasn't quite as late as Bøda had reckoned; time's pendulum swings so much slower in an empty house, the seconds so much longer and louder than the men's drunken laughter below. On she hurried after the hounds, hoping none of Dav's mates would spy her hiking off this late, though not quite as late as she'd figured. She didn't want their soused tongues to wag; this was a *hiatus*, an *interlude*, an empty threat, not a *real* split from Davvy. She didn't need folk gossiping her into a true break-up, no sirree. So she *hurried*.

The seafarer's moon was low and full—Bøda could see her way just fine, thank you—but the path was slippery with brine and midsummer showers. One misstep, that's all, one slight miscalculation and she was down on her arse, slipping and sliding on the winding path, now near the top, now suddenly close to the bottom, and there she went tumbling o'er the edge. Barely six feet yawned between her and the ground below, but it was enough to give her a solid jolt when she landed, and the momentum to spill halfway down the seawall's rune-scribed slope. When at last she scraped to a stop, tide lapping her toes, her nightie was torn filthy, her face a pink blub of shame. The fats of her palms a bloody mess.

What happened next is a blur of tears and strange alchemy. Bøda remembers the salt-glimmer of ancient symbols on the stone beneath and behind her. She recalls scootching up and up, away from the wet, then resting atop the wall's ramparts. She can still feel the sting in her pride, in her hands. Arn and Cú jostling her elbows, pressing warmth into her sides, refusing to give her an inch while she wept. Then, as always, she took comfort in the honest weight of wool in her lap. The soothing click-clack of her needles. Earlier that morning, Bøda had been knitting a charmed lie into the pattern of Davvy's soon-to-be best and only gansey. With chevrons, braids, a complex druid's circle at the yoke, she'd told yarns of his trawler o'erflowing with salmon. His profits transforming into a prize-winning fleet. His compass rose pointing true north. She'd knitted him a long life of joy, blessings, luck in love. Mirth and merriment and a fruitful marriage. But there on the seawall, she'd yanked it all out. Started again.

That night, blood-palmed and blubbing, she'd conjured a new design for her b'y while their loyal dogs snored beside her and seafolk splashed in the shadows of the Shillingate Isles. Dark tails sliced darker waters while Bøda knitted and cabled and purled. Slick-shining bodies rendered weird patterns on the sea's surface, each stroke at once sinuous and monstrous and mesmerizing. Enthralled, Bøda traced their merrish movements as she worked. Gaze at half-mast, she fashioned a similar, fey-fibred version of Davvy, casting him slantwise in the warp and weft of this new gansey while, before her, the cold creatures swam.

Gradually, one of their ilk emerged from Bøda's ichor-slick needles. The muck of her hands snagged on the strings, tugging wool-Davvy's torso out of shape. The shag of her blanket-cloak tangled with the skeins netted in her lap; with each stitch, Bøda's fingers caught and twisted real-Davvy's fine-as-flax locks around and around the strands of his knitted form. Not her *finest* work, she'd thought, long hours that felt like short minutes later, but it had felt *so good* making it, so *cathartic*. Skewed and speckled and rune-spattered, it was the fairest story she'd known how to tell. Oh, the left sleeve was wonky, the right not even started, but the sweater's back panel was done and the front only wanted a waistband. It was an important story, she'd thought, eyeing the finned silhouette of Davvy she'd cobbled out of grief and fury: the streaming hair and angular profile; the kinked waist and webby arms; the incomplete tail scraggling like tentacles from the ragged hem, spilling into her bag. A tanglesmithed tale of her b'y's flitting and flirting and floating around. A sweatered spell of his unfulfilled promise.

And every unfinished bit of it, she knew, would always be perfectly, horribly true.

'Waste not, want not,' the magpies peck from above as Bøda flings the last of her apples into the sea. Quick as chance, she snatches Cú by the scruff *right* when the pup's tensed to leap. Arn's a much lazier beast— far as he's concerned, it's table-service or starvation for him—but the red devil's not afraid to get *her* fur wet. She'll fish any soaked snack from the wash, hog that she is, and frighten off the finfolk while she splutters and chomps and slops.

'Gods!' Bøda wrenches a yelp out of Cú, shoving her into a sit. 'Stop it! For once, just *stop*.'

The bitches bray at that, of course they do, but Bøda keeps her chin down. She kisses an apology into Cú's wiry crown, ruffles her short ears, gets a lick for her efforts. *If only it was that simple. Fault and forgiveness.*

Oh, what an ordeal it had all been. Finding Davvy awaiting *her* at home for a change, but not how she'd ever wanted, not how she'd dreamed. That night, he'd gasped to see her, Bøda had thought, he'd gasped at her newfound knitted calm, maybe even at her generous beauty as she'd stood there, starlit and magnanimous in the doorway, the wronged woman returned and ready to absolve—but no, *oh no*—he was gasping, gasping, *gasping* for breath—*Davvy!* she'd cried—his blue-black mouth gaping and nostrils squeaking, the rook-nose Bøda loved reduced to a handsome ornament—*Davvy, I'm here!*—his gills flapping uselessly, filtering nothing but fear—*Oh, what have you done* —his green eyes bulging, the whites glowing, phosphorescent—*What have you done*—the bedsheets slick where he lay, slimed and syruped from all his flopping and flailing—*Oh Davvy, hold on*—his tail orca- thick at hip and haunches but ragged at the ends, a fish-skin fringe where natural-born merfolk wore fully-fleshed fins. *Hold on now, Davvy*, she'd cried, running to their pallet, shuddering at the kinked waist and webby arms, then bending to shoulder him like a stolen bride. Her hefty seafarer was suddenly light as a sand dollar—*Davvy, oh Davvy*—all fishbone and white meat now, no more passionate, stupid, silly, darling, dumb man—*oh what have you done*—just a creature of scale and story.

He'd blacked out before Bøda quite reached the lookout, where old man Calhoon had been slumped on the bench with a crock of screech in one hand and his grizzled head in the other. Lord knows Davvy'd be driftwood and dust now if Jezzie and May's grog-swilling Da hadn't helped Bøda roll her sorry b'y into the sea.

Pulse still jacked from the effort of getting back down here again, Bøda grunts as she shoves Cú behind her, away from the ocean's grasp, the crooked darkness slithering just below the surface. One by one, the apples she'd thrown *plip* out of sight. Bøda's thin lips wrinkle. Won't be more than a minute now, she guesses; he's taken the bait. Quietly humming, she takes up her needles, pulls Davvy's near-knitted gansey from the netting, pins the sack between her elbow and ribs to free her hands. Night after night, she gets a feel for this wool's odd tension, fingering the long blond hairs still matted into the rune-rusted yarn before setting her whalebones a'clacking. Sometimes Bøda fancies there's a tingle in her forearms then, a lingering trace of Davvy's limp tentacles clinging the way they had that night, as she waved Old Calhoon off home and flumped flat on her belly to plunge her sweet legless b'y into the drink, holding onto him for dear life. She knits around the memory of Davvy's shredded hindquarters slurp-sliding on her warm skin, clammy ribbons coiling around her wrists as he went under, as he sank into the deep, as he swam off—but not *away*.

Not for good.

Not yet.

Maybe not ever.

A white geyser of bubbles breaks the surface while Bøda tightens the fresh rows she's just added to Davvy's sweater. She glances at the roiling water. Returns to the new tangle she's worked. Hard to miss the *oomph* even this extra bit of length has lent his tail-power. Imagine the speed he could muster if she crafted him proper fins, shapely flukes, a streamlined end to his story? Imagine how fast he'd be then! How far he'd be able to go.

Bøda sighs and rips out the rows.

'You must be cold,' Davvy says after shaking the sea from his dreadful locks, words whistling through pointed teeth. Bøda winces at his piercing voice, his ungainly stroke. Above water, her lad's awkward, entirely graceless. A tadpole with ill-fitting flippers. Bøda has tried to fix it. She *has*. More than once. The skein for Davvy's right sleeve rests snug in her sack; his merrish right arm's listless without it, a silk stocking with no limb inside. And the full strength of his rudder is strung, right now, right here, on her needles. All she has to do is finish it. Tie those knots. Cast off.

More than once, she's made a start.

It's just—

'Nobody warms you like *I* do,' Davvy says, eeling himself o'er to the seawall. He looks up at her, dimples a grin. 'Come on, love. Give me a leg up.'

Bøda swallows, hard, as his unspoken *please*. At his forced flippancy. She toys with the wool, clicks off a dozen stitches to soothe her nerves. It should be easier by now, shouldn't it? Healing. Recovering. Starting again. Every day she considers doing it, cutting away the blood-stained yarn, unwinding the misshapen sweater, correcting the hair-strung design. *So easy*. Even now, again, Bøda slides the wool free. She unwinds the flawed tail on Davvy's gansey. Undoes his wool-self up to the navel. Watches as he braces flesh and bone against the symbol-scrawled barrier, his good arm straining, jaw clenched and gills pumping. What fine legs Bøda might give him instead. Strong and lean, spun from good clean wool, long legs to wrap all the way around her, proud legs to walk her down the aisle—

'I won't leave you,' Davvy manages between strangled gulps. It should be so easy, Bøda thinks, reading the pain in his expression, scared and hopeful and stubborn, so easy to do what he wants. To knit them back into their old patterns. To knit him back together. But—

'You know me, Bøda,' Davvy says. 'You know that—'

The spoiled Stagg vixen's painted snout pokes o'er the cliff's edge, cherry lips catcalling at them from above. 'Hey, Bød!' *Boooood*. Instinct or bad sense lifts Davvy's head. Is that another dimple? Is that a smile? He blinks, puckered mouth curling at the tart's attention. 'Sure this in't the one that got away?'

Davvy's gaze anchors down to Bøda.

'I won't ever stray,' he says, desperate now, and true.

'Of course not,' Bøda says. 'I know.'

Oh, how the bitches snort then. How they *howl*.

'Plenty more fish in the sea!'

Let them laugh, Bøda thinks, her needles swift as revenge. *Click-clack*, the gansey-lad once more wears a wool tattertail, *click-clack* the merrish b'y squirms at her feet, wailing on the seawall, fillets splayed and frayed and trailing, *click-clack* he slips back into the gloom, a keening froth of frustration and woe.

Let them stare. Bøda snaps once for the hounds. *Let them talk.* She sheathes her needles in the balled-up hanks of sweater, bags her hardest work. Jagging her hands across the salt-rimed runes, she grits her teeth. Gathers her wits. Draws blood.

To th'abyss with them, Bøda thinks, retracing her steps to the viewpoint. Spitting curses into the glowering dark. *To th'abyss with them all.*

A SHOT OF SALT WATER

Accordions unpleated welcoming songs the day the mermaids returned.

The first notes droned joyful at dawn, played by young men with wool collars unrolled against the wind. Mattress-clouds bulged above land and water, miles of damp cotton dulling the fishermen's music. As the sky blanched, fiddlers sawed harmonies, horsehairs screeching on weather-warped bows. Bodhráns were rescued from blanket boxes and cupboards, clatter-spoons from the backs of junk drawers. Soon drummers thumb-pounded down autumn-gold slopes from the village. Beats jigged and reeled past the wharves, along the coast, then splashed through froth seething to shore.

Sparking a cig, Billy Rideout watched the procession from the dunes. Nodded at the lack of flute-wailing. That hollow music wasn't fit for a homecoming, he thought. Too much like drowning-storms. Like last breaths blown through old bones.

There'd be singing later, in Ma Clary's kitchen. And in the tavern. In the shipyards. Up and down the waterfront, men were already warming throats with liquor and oil, preparing for tonight. Mermaids liked a bit of haze in his tenor, or so Billy-Rid told himself, sucking smoke.

Half a day's sail away, the first tall masts striped the gunmetal surf.

'Get your arse down here, Rid,' called Eli Stagg from the strand, carrying an armload of tinned gooseberries. 'Grab a basket on the way.'

Billy-Rid pocketed the half-burnt stub, did as told.

On the beach, musicians and local b'ys milled. Horsing around between tunes, they swigged from jars while uncles and grandys set up trestles. Ankle-deep in the shallows, ancient sea-salted women supervised, criticising with squints and scowls but few words. Pointing out which tablecloths needed pinning down. *Tsking* at the smell of charred griddle-cakes. Snapping knot-knuckled fingers as Billy-Rid made a mess of the buffet, jumbling savouries and sweets on the boards. Between snorts, the matrons snacked on baked haddock. Sucked on bottles of spiced rum, dipper, screech.

'Full sail,' said the eldest, her white hair still plaited in maid's ropes. Keen eyes trained on the horizon, she talked around a half-chewed wad. 'Fleet's racing the rain.'

Innards clenched, Billy-Rid pretended not to see the sharp-nosed schooners spearing closer. Distant fuzz-dots slowly hardening into crows-nests, smudged lines into hemp ropes. Coffin-dark jibs fading to shades of burgundy and mud on approach.

Beneath the proud sails, tall figures flitted to and fro on deck. They climbed the rigging, easy as flies. They swung the boom. They white-waked it for home.

Rid turned away, fumbling a plate of currant loaves. Gulls swooped, crammed their gullets with sweet white bread, as rowboats were lowered over gunwales a mile off shore. Ducking to avoid claws and beaks and wings, the b'ys each took up a shot of salt water.

'Fill yer guts,' they said, tossing it back for luck.

'Good lads,' said the nans, shooing the squawkers. Smirking when Rid suggested a second shot.

'Only takes one,' they said.

'Better safe,' Billy Rideout replied, upending another glass. Failing to drown the squirm in his guts.

The mermaids far outnumbered their rowboats, neither so many as when they'd first set out.

Clinker planks and women both were hard-worn from their travels. Hulls were mottled, keels paint-flaked. Otter-skin slickers were ripped and sleeveless, showing off oar-muscled arms. Canvas pants were ragged, storm-chewed at the hems; some hung like skirts, revealing tattooed thighs. Short-straw girls remained out on the ships—so close but still so far from home. Guarding the profits of their time abroad, the yield of raiding and trading. Scoping the waters for ill-omened shadows.

The shore party leapt overboard, hauled tired skiffs from hard-packed to soft sand. Their hair was dreadlocked, rimed with spray. Ten months at sea had staved in their cheeks, chiselled the roundness from hips and breasts. Blubber-treated packs were slung cross-body, leaving their arms free for fighting. Several hefted short-swords, others had daggers—though weapons weren't needed for *this* landing. There were no screams at the seafarers' approach, no terror at the sight of harpoons. Instead a baritone chorus whooped its greetings, singing tunes that beckoned them, one and all, inland.

Blood-cracks split the maids' smiles as they ran to their dads, their b'ys, their lovers. Only one made the trip from water to welcome slowly. Concentrating, stepping carefully, she waddled across the flats with buckler-strap loose around a misshapen belly.

'Reckon your lass is carrying,' Ma Clary said to Billy-Rid, lifting her pipe at the girl he loved. Then the old sailor bent, knees cracking, and palmed a handful of shells off the strand. Whispering a blessing, she threw the lot like confetti. 'First time lucky.'

'Lucky,' said Rid's mouth, while the rest of him gaped. Sweat pricked his brow, despite the chill air. The sky puckered and began to spit.

Lord look at her, he thought, fumbling for a stiff whiskey to keep him upright. For nigh on ten months—a whole season's sailing—he'd packed every minute with distraction. Full days on the wharf, full nights at Kelloway's pub. Cod-fishing, carousing, pickling his brain. Trying not to think of this moment. Of her.

Alberta Stagg.

His Beetie.

Lord *look* at you, he thought, lungs floundering. His gaze skimmed the cords of Beetie's flaxen hair, the many hoops in her ears, the welts around her knees, the mermaid-cut of her calves.

Just look at you, he thought, and look he did; returning, again and again, to the bulge slung at his girl's waist. The bundle cloak-shielded from the elements, the spatter now a steady drizzle. *She's carrying*, Ma Clary had said—and so she was. Hefting a child Billy-Rid might have given her. A baby she might have gone and got for them both.

They ate everything the gulls hadn't scabbed, drank til the rain seemed a joke. Gingham blew off tables, cartwheeled into the waves. Crocks were dropped, broken, buried under the skip and twirl of dancing feet. *A waste*, potters would say the next morning, but for now these losses were celebrated. They were expected. Annual tributes to the gods of wind and water.

Rum doubled Billy-Rid's vision, ale blurred its edges. Swept into the sodden crowd, he swigged from any jar that passed. One minute he was on the sand, numb legs failing to reach Beetie three tables over; a blink later, he was reeling up the path into town, beach at his back. He was battered and tossed onto the road leading to Kelloway's, a flurry of strong palms beating across his shoulders as the other b'ys tried to slap up some of his fortune.

'Filled her guts,' they said, all ruddy-cheeked, butcher-built men like himself. Thumping and clapping, the lads passed him shot after shot of salt water, whooping til he threw them down, howling when he threw them back up. Leaving Rid to contemplate the mess on his boots, they stomped up the planks to the pub. The din inside roared when the double doors opened: slurred voices, shrill pipes, the barman shouting out orders. Before they swung to, Billy-Rid heard the b'ys cheering his mermaid. And quieter, but distinct, Beetie's giggled delight as the babe in her arms started baying.

Might be they're right, Rid thought, straightening. The kid *could've* been my doing. It happens. It has happened.

Stumbling, he took a step toward the pub for each of the land-births they'd had on this rock they called home. Beetie was one, no doubt about it; not a snip or surgeon-scar on her. But that was eighteen-odd years ago, he thought, shaking the rum-fog from his head. Ma Clary's niece? Yeah, she and the bottleman from Bonnebay had themselves a small brood of landlubbers. No gills, no fins in the bunch. Half a dozen of Rid's dockside mates were earth-stock, like him; no merchild he'd ever seen could grow *their* class of beard or bulk.

Not every babe was fished, Rid thought. He paused on the stoop, listened. This one *could* be mine.

Inside, the baby cried, a liquid mewl with a note of whale-song about it.

Alberta had once been Billy's alone, his own shy girl who'd beet-blushed at his swagger, his attention, his gut-twisting love. She'd been his long before her summer-ship weighed anchor. And everyone knew he'd been hers.

As was custom, he'd ringed a reef-knot of silk round Beetie's finger, making their intentions plain.

As was custom, he'd knotted his body around hers, morning and night, making the most of Spring.

As was custom, when her bloods kept coming despite Rid's best efforts, when the tides changed and currents warmed, when the cannery reeked to the high heavens and barley began greening the fields, his Beetie had bodied the very schooner that had carried her back again today, carrying.

It wasn't *that* long ago, Rid thought, pushing into a blue fug, heavy as the clouds outside. The guppy *could* be ours.

On the pub's threshold, he stopped, fought for breath. The air was humid with merriment and music. Standing on chairs near the hearth, Dana and her water-born son added banjos to the fiddlers' medley. Over at the bar, Vin Clary out-plucked them all on his mandolin.

Harmonicas jangoed between verses, competing with the lonesome burtle of uillieann pipes. Between cups and jars, hands pounded stained barrels. Heel-rhythms had the floor quaking, pleasure thrumming across puddles trekked in with the rain.

At the room's heart, Beetie was surrounded by cheek-pinchers, back-thumpers, drunken coo-cluckers. Her fair hair browning with sweat. Broad face living up to her nickname. Rawhide jerkin unlaced, revealing a strong collarbone and the kelp necklace she'd made for their tying day. Billy-Rid fancied the links still had some wet to them, though the roe-beads had well and truly dried. The little gems were grey, now, as the pebbles in her gaze.

Meeting it unsteadily, he flubbed a grin. A tiny hand had reached up from within Beetie's vest, its blunt fingers groping for the seaweed chain. Hard to tell from this distance if the bluish cast of its skin was more than a trick of grog-tinted light. If its little digits had been tipped with nails, or anemones. If it looked anything at all like him.

Don't go, he'd wanted to beg, all those months ago. Beetie had woken hours before dawn. Her gear waited by the front door; it hadn't taken long for her to dress, to shoulder a hooded harpoon. The weapon had been a gift from her da, the blades vicious, star-shaped. The same one her late mam had wielded. It suited her, Rid had thought, but couldn't bring himself to mention it. Beside him, the pillow still cupped the space where Beetie's head had rested. The linens were still soft with her warmth. Billy-Rid had inhaled the beeswax scent of her, refusing to get out of bed, to say goodbye.

I can be enough, he'd wanted to lie. *We have more than enough, with us two.*

Instead, he'd whistled for fair winds and Beetie had turned a pretty crimson, self-conscious in her new skins and leathers. It was her first voyage, her first chance to hunt and shoal and multiply. She would have gone with the mermaids no matter what he'd said.

He only wished he'd said more.

'Good on you, lad,' Eli Stagg said now, full-proud with drink. Rid's teeth rattled as Beetie's old man threw an arm round him. Nodding thanks, he wriggled free only to be swept away in a current of dancers. The music capered, tempo unpredictable. Suddenly Billy-Rid was gripped under the pits, lifted like a child, then twirled and twirled and twirled. Lanterns pitched overhead, shadows tipsy. Awash in the stench of wet wool, beer and eel, Rid swooned. Clipped his chin on someone's sharp elbow. Bit his tongue. Saw stars.

''Bout time,' Beetie said, yanking him straight. Herself nearly tall as he, even barefoot. The hand she'd extended streaked red with rope-burns. Her laugh sun-bleached, voice barnacled. 'Thought you were avoiding me.' She glanced down at the gup. 'Us.'

''Course not,' Rid said, barely hesitating.

Uncertainty flickered across Beetie's face—half a second's flinch—but she squashed it with a pickled-egg kiss. Almost a year at sea had livened her tongue but sapped its honey. Billy-Rid recoiled.

'Aren't you going to introduce us,' he said, too stiffly. Trying again, he wiped his mouth and dimpled at the mermaid, his once-darling girl.

'Go on then,' Rid prompted, as the musicians mopped their brows, drained the dregs of Kelloway's black ale. A few began packing their instruments, aiming to reach Ma Clary's before the crowds. 'Let me see it.'

'*Her*,' Beetie said, pulling back the sealskin swaddling.

No quick-mustered charm could keep the pleasant in Rid's expression. His smile-muscles went slack as paste.

'Gorgeous, isn't she?'

Fronds of skin dripped from the bub's angled jaw, waxen flaps the hue of new leaves. Her chest jutted as she grizzled, the strakes of her ribs visible through a thin smock. The arms were slender but stunted; fern shoots partly unfurled. Rid took in the equine nose and winced at the strange list of her gaze. One deep brown eye turned up at Beetie; the other swivelled its iris 'round at him. Translucent lids blinked independently, or not at all.

Billy-Rid searched for signs of gills, for coronet bumps on the fry's skull, found none. Yet.

Beetie beamed. 'Isn't she the prettiest little thing you ever saw?'

Around them, mermaids raised jars, bellowing shanties. Kelloway tapped the last keg, uncorked the final two barrels of mash. Tin pipes whistled for all the luck in the world, their empty wind blowing beautifully nowhere.

'Never seen one quite like her,' he said at last, earning another strong-armed embrace. The stolen bub pipped and squirmed between them.

Quivering, Rid buried his face in his wife's brackish locks and wept.

For a month they called her Guppy, same as every other sea-child. A month for her to earn a name, to thrive on land. A month for Billy-Rid to adjust.

Drinking mostly brine, the bub grew plump and fast.

While Rid nursed the thirsty thing, Beetie and the mermaids disappeared over the rim of the world. Twice daily, fish drew them oceanwards and fish brought them back. The routine kept the town's pantries full, the lasses' figures hard. Before long they'd be pointing bowsprits east again, raising sails, whetting harpoons; until then, the women would work. Keep the iron in their muscles. It wouldn't do for the island's best hunters to run to suet in the off-season. It took steel to replenish stocks.

Billy-Rid knew this as well as anyone.

Folk wouldn't survive without them.

With the b'ys at Kelloway's, Billy-Rid laughed it off. His failure. He was no different from his mates, really. None of them had managed to cast their lines through a mermaid's salt—except Tuck, just that once, when he'd barely learned how to handle his rod. That kid hardly counted, though. Within a day, the poor thing suffocated with a bellyful of air.

Even so.

By now Beetie must've been raw as Rid was, after a fortnight of his contributions. His trying and trying and trying for a bub of their own.

A *real* one.

One *he'd* made, not one she'd snatched.

Maybe the sea had grown too strong in Beetie's blood. Maybe, or too weak in his. Maybe it was the way she rode him now, as she never had before. Maybe it was the bile in Rid's thoughts, the burn of wondering where *exactly* she'd got the gup, from whom *exactly*, and *how*. Maybe it was the ache of not-asking.

Maybe it was that Beetie didn't—wouldn't—need him.

Maybe that's what left him so empty.

The gup's not right, Rid thought.

All afternoon on the quay, she'd huffed and chortled in Ma Clary's lap, gumming a piece of dried cod. The gran doted on Beetie's girl, watched after her while Rid sorted and cleaned and filleted a half-ton of trout. When name-day planning had called Ma up to the bingo hall, she'd passed the bub on to the coastguard. Taking turns, the young men harnessed Gup to their backs, buoyed by her weird fluting as they patrolled the harbour. At last, when no one else had been free, Billy-Rid was forced to bring the baby and her noise home.

The cottage had been dank as a bait-house when they'd got in— Beetie'd had the windows open again, despite the autumn squalls. Rid hadn't bothered to sop the puddles beneath the casements, knowing they'd soon be propped and dripping again. Beetie claimed to like it that way, cool and blustery. Said it reminded her of being on deck.

Rid lowered the baby into clean bathwater, then dragged the tin tub near the hearth. Hunkering beside it, he sat back on his heels. Paddled his fingers down by Guppy's feet, avoiding the spiked-curl of her toes. She sputtered strange notes, maw agape.

As if it hasn't mastered its nostrils, Rid thought. As if the damp air up here is too dry for its mouth.

With one hand he soaked a square of flannel, wrung it out, soaked and wrung, soaked and wrung, splashing himself more than her. The other cupped his chin, held his head up. Orange pennants rippled in the flue-draft, tips jigging, hooking Billy-Rid's lashes, dragging his lids to half-mast. Logs sighed and settled. Heat lulled like nostalgia, like sun-baked memory.

In the yawning flames, Rid saw golden days; time he'd spent with Beetie *before*. When there'd been no ships or guppies for them. No bucklers or harpoons. No tying ceremonies or name-days. No bub that wasn't theirs, not really. When they'd been kids, and sweet on each other. When they'd taken shifts at the guttery together, quick-slicing salmon bellies, carp heads. When they'd snuck to the rock pools at lunch, smoked stolen cigs. When they'd decorated each other's faces with iridescence, scales stuck to their overalls, and they'd pretended— Lord how they'd pretended—they were magical.

She was, Billy Rideout thought, now as then. Salt glistening in her hair. Freckles on her nose, blue and yellow in the sunlight. *The chunk torn from her gums an inheritance,* Ma Clary once said, *of the first mermaid, the first hook that failed to snag her. It was the second cast that had done the trick, taken the girl home.*

The second cast, Rid thought, up to the elbow in suds and warmth. The second had been strong and true . . .

'What the blight are you doing?'

At the cottage door, Beetie dropped her cloak and bag. Cold night gusted in as she dashed across the small room. Five strides and she'd shoved Rid away from Guppy, the bub burbling, submerged to the nose.

'A splash in the basin is more than enough,' Beetie said, scooping the child, voice lowered, aiming to soothe. '*More* than enough. You don't want her to drown.'

Of course not, Rid thought, sinking to the floor. Beetie slapped his hands when he reached for a towel. Cooing and fussing, she turned her back. Swaddled the girl tight, held her close. Bounced the near-miss from her nerves.

Left eye trained on Rid, right on the overfull tub, Guppy keened. A rippling, uncertain song.

Oh, how the b'ys would snort to see Billy-Rid acting so mawkish.

Steaming Gup's bottles, scrubbing her unders, airing quilts between downpours. Plumping Beetie's pillow with fresh-plucked down. Roasting stones in the fire, slipping them under the blankets, keeping the ice from her toes while she napped. Bartering crayfish for spuds, onions, carrots; sweet-talking Ma Clary out of a vat of new cream.

Cooking huge batches of the Staggs' favourite chowder. Bypassing Kelloway's in the evenings, heading straight home to see Beetie off to the docks. Waking early to greet her at dawn. Brewing new leaves for her after-sail tea.

The week leading up to Gup's naming-day party, Billy-Rid did what he could. To help. To make things right. He threaded garland after garland of urchins, ribbons, coral, and kelp. He hung them from the bingo hall's rafters so Beetie wouldn't have to do it. He lugged tables and benches galore, set them all up, leaving plenty of room for dancing. When Kelloway came to stock the bar, he stayed the hell out of the way.

But still.

Even so.

Beetie had stopped tangling her legs 'round his at night. She'd started bringing Guppy with her down to the docks. Saying: the nans loved the girl so. Saying: they cared deeply and dearly. Saying: they wanted nothing but to spend time with the child.

'It would be cruel to deny them,' Beetie said, freeing Guppy from Rid's grasp. 'They're only trying to make her feel welcome. They're doing their best.'

As if Rid wasn't.

That night, Kelloway's overflowed with rum and revellers. The whole town was expected to show the next morning, bow-tied and be-gartered, before mermaids lifted anchor for the first catch. But a naming-day just wouldn't be a naming-day if folk weren't fur-tongued and skull-sore, retching into the buckets Billy-Rid had scattered around the hall. The whole island was expected at dawn: sea-striders and sand-runners, tykes and cane-toters. Those born to men, and those taken.

Every last soul would *have* to be out of their blimmin senses come morning, to pretend that Guppy belonged.

'Limber up,' Rid said to Eli Stagg, flexing and throwing back another belter of screech. His words burred, slow in coming. 'Got a big ask tomorrow.'

One minute Beetie's da was tilting the rim, the next his glass was drained on the bar in front of an empty seat. Rid's neck swerved. A pint foamed in his grip. A second later it was shards glinting beneath his stool, replaced by a plastic kiddie-cup. Black mash and sour-cherry swilled down his craw, scorching a path to his stomach. Behind the taps, Kelloway scowled as Billy-Rid ordered another, but served it up anyway.

'Good man,' Rid said, or something like. Maybe, 'Lucky man.' The barkeep leaned over the counter, lit the cig Rid had stuffed arse-end into his gob. The publican never had gups of his own, lucky man, never had planted nor sea-sowed. Good man.

'How about a splash of the bland stuff,' Kelloway said, sliding a pitcher of melted ice down the plank. 'Might be you've had enough of the harsh.'

'Might be,' Rid agreed, but it felt good in him, the blaze in his heart, the lava in his belly. It got him up off the stool, onto the dance floor, where Beetie spun and spun, locks flying loose, baby on her hip. Squeezeboxes hawed and fiddles wheezed as Rid barged through the crowd. Flutes, real flutes, no mere ha'pennies these, tootled like Gup as he wrenched her away from the mermaid. His wife.

'Thing's squawking for a feed,' he said, cradling the bub. 'Look how thirsty—'

'Give her back.'

Around them, sailors thumbed knife hilts, toyed with sword belts. Pipers trilled, undaunted, while wooden spoons clacked, missing beats. String-pluckers and sawyers climbed off stage, tension bloating into the gaps of their music.

'She's thirsty,' he said quietly, enunciating precisely. 'I'll take care of her.'

Beetie rested her palm on Billy-Rid's forearm, firm but gentle. She smiled, a spark of fun in her expression. Humour he hadn't seen in weeks. 'Do what you gotta do, Billy-b'y,' she said, patting him like a child. 'But mind you keep her wee snorter above water this time.'

Through the hot rush of blood in his ears, Rid couldn't hear every mermaid's laughter. Only the one closest to him. The loudest and least shy.

Outside, threadbare clouds blanketed the navy sky. Stars peeped through holes here and there, silvering billows above and swells below.

Thigh-deep in the ocean, Billy-Rid crooned a lullaby. In his shaking arms, Guppy added garbled notes, high as the moon-chunk overhead. Its reflection hazed around them, wavering on the expanse of wet black. In the distance, dorsal fins broke the surface. Two. Four. Seven. Too rigid to blend with the whitecaps. Rid stood and watched like the sentries weren't; the men slunk off for a stint of elbow-raising down at the pub. *It's been a month*, they'd no doubt reasoned. *Surely a month gone is time enough for the damned fish to forget.*

Rid studied Gup's elongated features, saw their likeness cresting the waves.

Still singing, he trudged further into the wash. Winter lurked in the deeps, shrivelling him. Shame boiled anew, thoughts of Beetie scorching his cheeks. How she'd left him. How she'd returned.

The baby gurgled as Rid plunged her. In and out, in and out, in and out of the water. She giggled as if it was a game, her skin-fronds flapping and floating, dripping. Sodden, her mess-cloth sagged, slid off, sank. Switching tunes, Billy-Rid disentangled Gup from her smock, let her ridges free, the hard clay of her skin. All spine and cartilage and bone. Better, he decided. The bub honked, wide-gummed with agreement. More natural, he thought. The way she would've been for her naming-day dip come daybreak.

The sea foamed as Rid churned. Submerged or not, Guppy was alert, eyes ever open, ever swerving. Salt water rushed in and out; her protruding lips sucked, spurted. Hoarse, Rid hissed 'Come on, come on,' avoiding the bub's mouth-fountain. Her odd gaze. Its unblinking ease, its alien colour.

He played deaf to the squelch of liquid burps.

'Come on,' he repeated, louder now, holding the girl under.

Forearms straining, Rid whispered, 'Come on, come on,' as ten seconds passed, twenty, the baby's slow-wriggle turning full-squirm.

'Come *on*,' he said again and again, voice cracking, '*Come on*,' until, finally, she was wrenched from his grasp.

The creature was more man than seahorse, more stallion than pony. A trumpet nose dominated his long face; traces of sorrow in the round black eyes were undermined by the angry trumpeting of his snout. Spikes lined his muscular arms. Fronds the same shape and hue as the bub's dangled from a strong jaw. A carapace of ribs toughened his chest, accentuating the round softness of his stretch-marked belly. His were a warrior's shoulders: broad, ink-marked, boasting scars. Squiggles puckered the flesh on biceps and delts. A vicious, spark-shaped scab livid between clavicle and neck. Beetie's wound.

Treading water for a moment, the hippocampus cradled his squeaking child. Mesmerised by her existence. Tail curled around weeds, the creature stretched to his full height—shorter than Billy-Rid.

Our Guppy would've been quite the runt, he realised. From the looks of it.

The seahorse nipped gills into his baby's neck, then immersed her slowly, gently. As though afraid she'd vanish if let out of sight. As she was lowered, Guppy exhaled without music. Quietly grateful. The dissonant strain of her land-breathers hushed.

Not ours, Rid corrected as the bub drank the sea into her lungs. As she and her da sank into the star-speckled blackness, without a word. She was never ours.

Ripples arrowed east, flippers and arms slicing away toward plundered isles. Waiting for his pulse to slow, Rid tapped out the jig-splash of seahorses departing. When he could no longer tell the difference between liquid-peaks and fins, he turned and faced shore. Saw the yellow glow of Kelloway's atop the hill, spilling like weak ale across the boardwalk. Snippets of song drifted on the quickening breeze. Caws of joy. Back-slaps of mirth.

Shivering, Rid gauged the distance between *here* and *there*.

A far walk, he decided. Farthest he might ever take.

Wilting to his knees, Rid felt his limbs vaguely, steeped in chill. Just a minute's rest, he told himself, looking down at his freezing hands, flipping them a couple of times to make sure they were still there. On his palms, a swathe of scales shimmered in the moonlight. Had he touched the stallion? Had he soaked up some of his magic?

I must have, Rid thought. I must have.

Inspired, he sloshed to his feet. Shy Beetie always hated dancing and parties; he'd rescue her from the crowd, take her to the rock pools, freckle her pink prettiness with scales. Oh, how she'd glisten, then. How she'd love.

You're a fool, Billy Rideout, he thought a second later, flopping into the shallows. Part-squatting, he rubbed his hands together, watched the iridescence flake slowly away. His body aching with cold. Useless cock shrivelled. Balls in his belly. Overalls heavy with naught but seawater.

Only one way to fetch a bub, he knew. Only one that he could accept.

From the shallows, Billy-Rid swore he heard his wife's heels skip-stepping on Kelloway's floorboards. Emptied glasses thunking on the bar. Spoon-beats and hide-rappings and harmonica wails. Tilting his head, he listened to another, closer, deep-wooden rhythm. Tethered ships colliding with rails. Hulls bumping against pilings. Ropes creaking between gunwales and jetty. Masts swaying. Figureheads stretching, pointing to the fecund east.

Mind awhirl, Rid calculated.

He measured the span between *here* and way up the hill *there*.

Here and just over to the docks *there*.

Deciding, he bent and scooped a shot of salt water. Swallowed for luck. Steeled himself to go.

THE WIDOWS GUILD

Four thousand clicks north, home is a-calling. Its rasp-weathered voice trails the *Rambler*'s mermaiden crew—skilled seafarers all: harpoonists, netters, oar-pullers, sail-raisers, skin-divers, swashbucklers—and there's not a lass aboard deaf to its siren song, none immune to its forked-tongue tunes. Night and day, it croons of comforts they've nigh forgotten, hopes they've all but abandoned. Lonely beds wanting warmth. Magic half-stirred, half-spun, half-spoken. Scattergood's breakfast rolls. Cottages snugged in the dunes or ricketing high on breakwater stilts. Hotspring baths in winter to ease life's aches, polar bear swims to toughen them up at first thaw. Bells ringing young b'ys out to the Lundey to fetch a new flock of fine harpy brides. Casks swilling with Kelloway's deepest black screech. Bairns quickened inside their own bellies or hatched from hard shells or fossicked from hippocamp seas. Kin that await them, wearing their self-same features. Others that quite clearly don't.

Come, it beckons them—more often than not—come back to the shores that shaped you.

One more haul, the seamaids chaunt to the vast blue, pairing actions and words. Narrow feet a-slapping the brigantine's supper-clean decks, they thunder fore and aft across her worn planks, soles as bare as the tiny gilled babbies they've taken and tubbed in the hold. The ship's brightwork is spit-polished, her jibs and spinnakers set, slack lines tightened and made fast, square sheets a-billowing as the helmsmaiden steers them through coconut breezes.

Away! Away! Gybe through the wind, gals, 'til it gets good and sticky —then you'll know we're on the right track. One more haul to fill every last cradle and coffer. One more haul and we'll call it a day.

Aegis sings these lies loud and true like the rest of them.

There's no going back to the isles they've outlived, outloved, outgrown! Not now! Not tomorrow! Not *yet*.

One more haul, they cry in synchronous tune, drowning out home's insidious whispers. When the squall's up and the *Rambler* rolls like a red apple in a festival barrel, ducking and bobbing against the gale's greedy teeth, there's no time for stray thoughts. No worries about wee changelings left behind in lonely tidepools. No wondering if the gout-ridden blacksmith saw her out there that night, if he scooped the creature out of the wash, if he saved it. Gave it a chance. No, no, today it's *all hands! heave to! lie-a-try! keep her head six points from the wind!* It's salt-scouring speed to outmanoeuvre this gods-awful storm. It's rain lashing the crew's cheeks good and ruddy. Crows-feet clawing deep and deeper around their hard squints. Lips splitting with the fierce of their grimaces.

Light along! Aegis yells, her old knuckles cracking as she hoists heavy cables, legs steady despite everything. There's no place for the past in this toss-and-turn moment, not with the tempest tipping-and-toppling them, and that archipelago jutting up out of nowhere, that scattering of green cliffs and sheltering coves, and the grey waves tossing them landward. Rán's nasty daughters slip-and-slop them for hours, set on smashing the *Rambler*'s great hull to smithereens on sheer stone. Palms callused thick, Aegis lobs a hempen line overboard, gets its whale-bladder bumpers dangling portside, but it's not enough, not on its own; they'll need many more of these buffers to cushion the crash. Ever and always, the drift spins around her, so close she can taste it, but her focus is split—head, heart, hands—and she can't weave the world's currents alone.

Look ahead, Aegis cries, then cackles as Ruthena and Juniper

Hobble join her on the hawser—both strong as gorgons with their charm-dreads a-flailing—and together they balloon the ship's girdle so she fair bounces into this haven of a bay.

One more haul, says the captain when the storm's rage subsides, young Janny Magaw, her forearms muscled and gloved with blue tatts, mighty guns ever-flexing for more battle scars. As the sea simmers to turquoise, the sky burbles to blue and the clouds shred like sun-bleached cotton, the widows and witches and war-wives all survey the damage. Masts: straight as sequoias. Keel, oars, rudder: stalwart and ready. Figurehead: snarl-grinning and fluke gleaming, oaken gaze fixed far beyond the greatest map's margins. A single nod from Beetie Stagg's all it takes—*one more*, the first mate agrees—before they pull straws to see who can steal forty winks while she can.

Down the hatch to their hammocks, those sagging ghosts of unsleep clewed and slung from the deck's dark underside. Here the home-song wheedles like a demon—*remember feather mattresses? bedsprings? quilts?* —as the mermaids jitter into their narrow berths, tired to the bone but still buzzing with the thrill of survival. Some sluice their guts with sour grog, some sup on cold lamprey stew, some carve protection runes into the beams. Ritual, routine. *Another day done.* No time for bemoaning the thin canvas snugged around them, the chopped old clothes for padding and jute sacks for pillows, not when they've washed up here on the Harrower's Spars—an easy sail sunwards to Garnishee Reef, where the friskiest sea-stallions like to summer, their round bellies ripe with a fortune of fry.

One more haul, they whoop, while Aegis slinks further below the orlop deck and into the hold. So many of the maids' plans follow her down the companionway. *What about a pitstop at St. Jime's to raid the pearl harvest* (Ruthena's idea) *or we could shoot through Pelagica Strait* (this one's Beetie's) *to hunt rookie privateers*, but that won't do, it's too far off course, no matter how gallumphing and gold-clinking their galleons, *or let's head back to the* Dissent *and see what's left of her wreckage* (Juniper's suggestion, promptly boo-hissed) *or maybe a tour of the Great Garnet Isles* (says Sandolin, surprising no one) *where the liquor's hot, the masseurs dextrous, and the beaches are soft as butter!*

Lanterns swing from the gingerbread-work overhead—Captain

Janny always loves her girls gilded and frilly—dripping honeyed light onto the dozen half-casks splayed open between the steps and the stern. No portholes down here, just those low-hanging flames and the fey-shine swirling around Gladwin's fingers as she dabbles them in the tubs of cool brine. Aegis lifts her chin at the bosun crouched there in the aisle —along with the rigging and sails, it's Glad's duty to inspect and report on the state of their cargo—then creaks over to the makeshift nursery, all the while sucking in lungfuls of air thick with bilge-reek and algae. Submerged and lulled by the ocean's wavebeat, the three long-snouted babies they've obtained thus far don't seem to notice the stink.

No worse for wear, Gladwin signs up at her, knees audibly cricking as she straightens. With a satisfied sigh, she tosses a couple handfuls of kelp flakes into the water, then thumps Aegis on the shoulder. *Good chance this lot'll make it. If we're lucky*, she signs, squeezing past to rejoin the merrymakers, *they'll even thrive. And if we're* truly *lucky, the next haul will double our numbers—and won't the lasses be laughing then!*

Forcing a grin, Aegis unhooks a stool from the ceiling, hunkers down as the bosun monkeys up to the rollicking quarters. *We'll go 'round Cape Shoran*, comes a roar from above—sounds like Marelle's fully sloshing, then—*and then the southerlies can whisk our brave* Rambler *all the way back to the Rock.*

'Not long now,' Aegis whispers to the slumbering guppies and strokes their rubbery noses. Smiling as their tails bracelet her wrists, ring her fingers. Wasting more kelp in their tubs. Softly humming, she doesn't think of tidepools or starveling bairns. Eyes unfocused, she gropes for the drift—oh, so *close*—but only snatches a mindful of sorrow. One more haul, she thinks, scraping at tears. These wee foundlings are too thin, too delicate to survive, despite Gladwin's blithe assessment. They won't make it more than a month.

But the next ones might.

Or the next.

One more haul then, Aegis hums, before home.

DEEP IN THE DRIFT, SPINNING

A pause only Winnifletch herself notices, a twinge in her guts as she unsacks the gull that Gert Mews has lugged to her sea-spindle shack. Dazed but not dead, the bird crawks down onto her workbench. *Think of shearwater honey,* Winni tells herself, *with predictions truer than gold.* She grabs its fat fluttersome breast. Jams it wings-and-all between her vise's steel jaws. Holds firm. *Don't think of shattered sailors.*

Outside, free-gulls keen for their lost fellow, their lament high and lonesome, shearing through dark sheets of morning rain.

'You won't tell my mam?' By the hut's traitorous door, Gert gawps at Winnifletch like it's her own belly set to be crushed. The girl clutches a mickey bottle, empty of dipper and screech. Stormwater drips from her wool collar and hems, lanks her oat-coloured braids. On the woodstove a big iron pot's steaming, pipping and popping a tallow-stink tune. Gert wrinkles her nose, subtly covers her mouth. Thirty-odd noons into what should've been a sevenday simmer, the broth is festering, a carbuncle Winnifletch can't bring herself to lance. It should've been a brew to keep body and soul together. To keep her and Shale together.

It should have been.

'I've not seen your mam since she was your age, lass. Folk seek me, not t'other way round.' Winni pinches the gull's snapping beak. 'Still, you know the old saw: *word wings where it will*. Better it's you doing the saying, and soon, rather than some nosy flap-jaw.'

Sniffling as she warms, Gert scuffs a short path to Winni's side. Ducks under shell-and-nut garlands, kicks crab traps and half-knotted nets that're on the floor. Two steps from the hearth, she skirts around a rickety stool where Jinx craw-craws encouragement. Friend and familiar these past ten years, the old crow is a touchstone for Winnifletch, a nattering source of blue-black intelligence.

'This going to hurt?'

For the moment, Winni ignores her. *Think of sandpiper cider, its farsights sharp as a mermaid's harpoon.* Casting her mind into chance's currents, she focuses on the fates and fortunes floating around her. Senses more than smells the brine in their billows. The truths in their tickling breeze. *Think of plover milk, its tidings glad as birthday boys bound for the Lundey, rowing to fetch their first harpy wives from its cliffs.*

With a mental inhalation, Winni sifts the drift for the right whirl in the air, the right future Gert's here to imbibe. She draws everything in: these avian vessels, their airborne calls, their salt-spray scent. Magic, not marrow, will soon fill the gull's delicate bones. Magic to set them all flying.

'Sit, lass.' Without turning, Winnifletch takes Gert's bottle, slips and clips it below a funnel nailed under the workbench. Gert watches, wary of crow and conjurer both, then lowers herself onto the hearthstones, sighing as the woodstove heats her back. She can't have more than a year on Winni's own daughter—seventeen most like, eighteen at a stretch—but already she's bedded and wedded one of the Stagg b'ys. Already she's running their kin's haddock stall down at Barradoon harbour. Already she's growing some extra girth around the girdle.

But she's so naïve, this lass. So dependent. *You won't tell my mam?* So much *younger* than Shale, despite her age. *You won't tell?* How she snared a husband is no mystery—those pert looks, those pliable legs—but she's so *stupid*, clearly. Not believing her fish-smock's smaller now than it was several weeks ago, before her Stagg lad prowed north on the season's long trawl. Not trusting the new tune her body is singing, not daring to hear it on her own. Coming down to Winnifletch's cove instead of talking her troubles out with someone who loves her, asking for spells over her own mamma's insights. Stupid.

Only two things cause that slow-but-steady swell through a maid's middle—love and loneliness—and Gert has never wanted for company. Such a simple situation. Such a simple girl.

Although she's not said as much, not in so many words, Gert must've come here to water that bud in her belly. To soak and settle it, once and for all. To drink her fisherman happy.

That old rub.

'Hush now,' Winni says, anticipating Gert's unasked questions—they always have questions, her many door-darkeners, with their bagged birds and thirsty bottles—questions she can't and so doesn't answer.

Will it take long?

Will it go wrong?

Will it work?

Will it fix me?

So many uncertainties.

When is it my turn, Mam, Shale had asked, again and again. *Why won't you help me?*

Such scope for mistakes.

Don't think of silenced songpipes. Winnifletch firms her lips, concentrates. *Think of oldsquaw gladwater, its soft fizz a sure balm for sorrows.* There, now. Tension trickles from her heart into her hands. There it is: a gull-sized whorl in the ether, swirling just for Gert. With fingers and focus tight, Winni starts spooling it in. A tickle of doubt—*Don't think of Bear, blank, broken*—before the flow spins through her and into the struggling bird. Two, three firm twists of the vise's handle, long screws squeaking. With each turn, the gull's bones crack. Skin splits as the iron plates clamp together.

This time, Winni thinks, the drift is with her. This time the juice'll run good.

'A minute and you'll be on your way,' she promises. And this girl, this pretty, stupid girl, simply trusts her judgment. Trusts her experience. Trusts her.

In so many ways, she's nothing like Shale.

It's only this once that Gert Mews asks for Winni's help. And she hears her out. And she's here.

Shale's cleverness, her curiosity, would compensate for their isolation, Winni thought. Between the bottles and jars, the shelves in their shack were stuffed with books—fables and myths, natural histories and tales of adventure, biographies of the greatest mermaids Barradoon had known, tattlers about local harpies and sirens—and before Shale was old enough to fathom what any of it meant, Winnifletch read them all aloud, cover to cover, while she squirmed, while she watched, while she listened.

She'd thought their protected cove, their pebbled beach and their hut, was a world only big enough for them. But after a broken wing dropped Jinx onto their stoop, Winni let their small family grow, just that much and no more. Shale was smitten; the love between girl and crow bound them faster than any of Winni's spells or splints. Huge on Shale's lap, the crow abided her small pawings, her splay-fingered strokings, her pickings and pullings at that lustrous ancient black plumage. Jinx sheathed her beak when Shale peered into the bowl of mealworms Winni set out each morning; she waited for her to reach in and squish the fare first. And when Shale spread her wiry arms, burst out their only door to soar over their patch of dune-grass to the coast, Jinx was forever flapping beside her.

'Stay where I can see you,' Winnifletch called as her daughter dwindled. Shale splashed in the shallows, sang at the sun, such a soul-warming sight. 'Stay close.'

The crow calls Winnifletch back to the herring gull at hand.

Nectar drips from the carcass, a steady plink-plink-plink of drift-dew. As the phial fills, Winni channels the whirling in her gut, that full-flight feeling, that storm-toss'd and directionless drive, and *pushes* it into the mix.

The juice runs fast and free.

'There's your answer,' she says.

'I thought it'd be like steak-drippings,' Gert whispers, standing for a better look. 'But it's hardly red at all. That's good, right?'

'Not bad,' Winnifletch says, the liquid glowing like her kerosene lamp. Squinting, she holds it up to the window. Nods as wan light sparks off the glass, catching no flotsam or flaw in the brew. Blue-gold or red or netherworld black, as long as it does no hurt, they'll both be safe. As long as it does no harm.

She screws the cap on tight, all the while rattling off a market-list of do's and don'ts for the drinking. When she falls silent, Gert slips the bottle under her sealskin, jangles a small leather pouch onto the table, then repeats Winnifletch's instructions word for word.

'Just so,' Winnifletch says, half-expecting her to mangle phrase and juice both. Mistakes have been known to happen. Spindrift is wild and slippery as seaweed, no more hers to control than the tides. All Winni can do is focus. Catch what she can.

Will it work?

One thing she knows for certain: the tonic will be intense as the heart squeezing it. The dearer the wish, the more dangerous the water.

'Will it fix me?'

I can't fix what's not broken, lass, Winni thinks, that old ache seething inside her, that murmuration of regret. *There's nothing wrong with you.* Aloud, she mutters reassurances. Platitudes. Time heals all. Good things come. Nothing ventured. Out of habit, she plays to her strengths. Plays it safe. Small birds, small soothings, small sacrifices. No more, no less.

'Fair winds,' she says as Gert lifts her hood and turns for home. *Go talk to your mamma.* Head bent against the rain, Gert avoids the coast and instead makes for Shale's track through the dunes. Over and over, her hand returns to the new bulge under her slicker. Patting the proof of magic there.

And if this potion proves wishy-washy? Winni watches the rain sheer down from Gallahorn way, not liking Gert's chances of beating it to the Mews place. What if all she gets from this trip is a dousing? Well. Lasses always blame themselves first for such failures, don't they, finding

fault with their own minds and bodies when, truth be told, there is
none. Most lasses, anyway.

*Twice a year, mermaids' galleons sailed past Winnifletch's bay. What a
vision they made, so many tall ships with black pennants unfurled,
bowsprits spearing the horizon. Shield rims glinting above gunwales.
Glimpses of women commanding decks and rigging, featureless from this
distance, sure of foot and secure in their mission. 'Look,' Winnifletch
shouted, pointing at the carved vessels, their timbers oiled and gleaming.
'It's just like the stories.'*

Shale, small on the seashore, straightened. Shaded her eyes. Looked.

*Long before the armada curved out of view, she was stooped once more
in a clam-digger stance, scooping a series of holes in the sand. Around her
waist, one of Winni's aprons was folded and rolled, slung like a sailor's
luck-pouch, strings tying the leather into sections. One by one, the ships
slipped away behind her. One by one, Shale slipped oval rocks from her
makeshift pockets. A kiss and a cuddle for each precious egg, then she
carefully laid them, one by one, into the hollows.*

'Beautiful, aren't they?' Winni called.

*Cross-legged among her brood of stones, as varied and valuable as a
harpy's own clutch, Shale turned to her mother and smiled. 'Just wait 'til
they've hatched,' she said.*

Even as a tot, Shale sang little dirges whenever Winnifletch boiled up the
sevenday broths. Every third evening, it seemed, someone or another
came a-knocking with problems only a drift-spinner's juice could salve.
The Staggs and Corrigans, the Ridouts and Galloways—reluctant
regulars, bringing birds and bottles, taking Winni's advice, leaving their
troubles and good meat behind. Once they'd gone, Shale started up
again. It wasn't just the stench of marrow-melt that brought out the
banshee in her, nor the scald of fat sudsing around the cauldron's lip,

but the peeking and poking of beaks in the bubbles, the peeping and popping of tiny eyes.

'My poor sisters, Mither,' Shale would sob, hugging Winni's plump thigh, begging her to stop this particular cook-craft, ignoring her huffs and *don't call me that*s.

'That's *Mamma* to you, understood? Not *Mither*,' Winni corrected, again and again. 'I'm no harpy, lass.'

'But I am,' Shale cried, outstretching her skinny, featherless arms. Soft pink mouth pouting, cygnet face. 'I *am*, Mither. You just can't see it.'

Stop it, Winni wanted to snap, whenever Shale started singing that particular tune. *Listen to yourself*, she wanted to say, gaze rolling over the rafters. *Can't you hear what you're saying?*

Instead Winni cuddled her close, crooning to drown out the doubts.

You didn't make me right. I'm broken, Mamma. Fix me.

Now, spooning into her teeming pot the gannet carcass she'd just spun for Jerah Culvert, Winnifletch looks out the shack's sole window, hands and heart quaking as she stirs, as her mind roams. Across the storm-wreckage churned up on her beach, across riptides and white-crested chop, across the half-dozen miles (as the harpy flies) between her seething fire and all those cold nesting caves gouged into the Lundey's sheer cliffs. *How miserable it must be for harpy lasses out there*, she thinks. *Stuck in their shells all season, tucked in those awful nooks. Waiting and waiting for someone daring or daft enough to rescue them. To release them. To help them become—*

No, Winni had thought, still thinks. Tries not to. Her girl has seawater in her veins, doesn't she? A spirit shining bright as abalone shell. Shale is no delicate egg-husked creature, part bird and part girl. She's no prize for horny young b'ys to claim from Lundey Isle. Her hands aren't dainty and taloned, their tips polished useless and pretty; they're mermaid stock, aren't they? Blunt-built for roughing with spinnakers and stays, for monkeying up to the topgallants, for captaining crow's nests as she spyglasses wide waters for foes or foreign prizes. No *harpy*, her!

Especially not with a name like Shale, chosen for the double-prowed ship that had swifted her father in and out of Barradoon. Designed for hit-and-run raids, those longships, much like the fair-haired men who sailed them. Wave-wrangler that he was, he had moored long enough to frisk the chill from Winni's bed; short enough to avoid the by-blow.

He sure was something, Shale's da. Once.

Before—

Broth spits, scalding Winnifletch back to the fireside. The spoon slips from her grasp, sinks deep under foam and bones. She tongs it out, lays it to cool on the workbench, then dips in for a guillemot's ulna. Then what looks like a dovekie's radius. Then four scapula blades, each small as a tern's. Fused together *like so*—she sketches an imaginary arc with her eyes, sees the new wing-struts stretching high and strong as a pelican's—they might work on a bigger frame. They *could*. Maybe.

No, she thinks again, plinking shards and shafts back into the pot. It's too dangerous; such fancywork, such personal casting. A mermaid's life, with its boats and battles, is far better than any Winnifletch could ever stir up. Far safer than any potions she's pressed.

You could try, Shale used to beg. *Please, Mither. Please.*

Just try.

Call me Henny*, her daughter had said one day, dumping the dregs from Winni's brewpots.* ***Call me Soars o'er Stars****, she'd said, scrubbing blood from the vise—ancient as the Lundey, that name, a rare harpy title, but not right, not for Winni's stone-and-sea child.*

What's wrong with Shale?

Call me Starling or Sparrow or Crows-at-the-Sun.

What's wrong with the beautiful name I chose?

Call me Leda*, she'd said, after hearing some horrid story down at the wharf, some foolhood about girls and swans.*

You're missing the point on that one, lass.

No* you *are, Mither. *Flat refusing, from then on, to answer to Shale. Claiming flight and feathers suited her better than sails and ships.*

Only flighty part of Winni's girl was her fancy, she had thought then. Just look at those strong arms, that straight back, the stubborn tilt of Shale's dimpled chin. Look at those cords of salt-swept hair tumbling over her muscular shoulders, those blonde ropes begging to be twined with shell and silver charms. Put a deck under those tanned feet of hers, a harpoon in one hand and an oar and the other, and she was the perfect image of a sailor. A mermaid through and through. No doubt about it.

Except.

Fix me, Mither, *said not-Henny, not-Sparrow, not-Leda, again and again.* **Why won't you fix me? You conjured me up, a babe borne of moonlight and mud**—*that was a lie, of course; Winnifletch couldn't tell Shale the truth, not ever, about her father; not about his sleek ship and his round-the-world ways, not how he'd come here so proud and powerful, nor how he'd left Barradoon an awfully different man*—**so if your great magics made me, your great magics can save me.**

Oh the pleading, then, in not-Starling's ocean-glass eyes. **Help me, Mither. Help <u>me</u> for once, the way you do all of <u>them</u>.**

No, Winni had said, once too often, more than a month ago. **I love you too much, lass. I can't—**

Risk it, Winnifletch had said, twice. That was the second time, thirty-odd nights ago: right after Shale had stopped listening, grabbed her seal-skin and satchel, and slammed the shack's only door. The whole damned scene so familiar it ached. Much like the first time, there was Winnifletch gathering her ragged skirts, tripping over droplines and glass floats, jiggerpoles and trout bins in her haste. Choking on tears, chasing her love across the threshold, shouting from the stoop as a trail of footprints stretched away across the sand.

Risk it, she'd decided, sixteen years ago, heart and cleft throbbing from the wave-wrangler's fervent, oh-so-flattering attentions. Her Bear. What a way he'd had with hands and words! What a feast of friendship he'd offered, filling Winni right up before leaving.

So.

Come back, she'd yelled into the dawn wind, brandishing a newly full bottle, its pure garnet liquid flashing love-steeped promises. *Stay and your life will be rich.* A hexed swill of temptation her Bear couldn't ignore. *Stay and you'll know true bliss.*

Ignorance, Winnifletch thought now, recalling the wrong twist to Bear's face as he chugged the red cormorant draught. The empty flask thunking onto his otter-pelt boots, spit dribbling from his suddenly slack lips. The complete lack of interest when she'd cupped and kissed his wan cheeks. Only the click of his sun-whitened lashes blinking, blinking. The breath whistling in and out his dumb mouth. The vibrant, once-impish expression drooping into a dullard's stare.

Focus, she'd snapped, shaking him senseless there on the strand, *focus godsdammit*, knowing too late that *she* should have, when crushing that stupid bird, distilling and decanting its juice just for him; she was the one who'd needed *focus!*

If only she'd kept her head when spinning that drift, Bear wouldn't have lost his. If only she'd thought less of their far-travelling future together, more on happiness here at home, he'd have drunk himself into her life for good instead of out of it altogether. If only she'd wrung into that bottle all the love he needed, all the love she could give, instead of thinking of all she could take...

Hindsight, she'd thought, spiriting Bear back to his boat. Weeping over the wreck she'd wrought, the ruin she'd made of that once-lively rover. Too late, she'd thought, setting her lover's body on the thwarts, wrapping his limp hands around the oars, setting him silently adrift. Lesson and limits learned.

So.

Come back, she'd hollered, sixteen years and a month ago later, as Shale trudged away, over the dunes. *Please come back.* This time holding nothing but hope that her daughter would hear her, that she'd change her mind and come back. That she'd unfix her fantasies from Lundey Isle and its barnacled nesting caves. That she'd leave their skiff moored where it was, right here in their sheltered cove, where she was no harpy but always Winni's own little girl. Safe and loved and *whole*.

Fix me, Mither.

I can't risk it, Winnifletch had said. The drift's spin was too erratic, too unpredictable, too turbulent to hitch on Shale's impossible dreams.

It would only smash them like paperbark boats on Gutterson's Reef, leaving everything—and everyone—broken.

I love you too much, Winni wanted to tell her. *So I can't.*

The day Shale left, Winnifletch had started mixing what should've been the biggest, most potent sevenday broth she'd ever brewed. Hands and heart adding ingredients on their own, fate finding all the right fixings. Bitters to bind and herbs to heal. Jaegers and phalaropes crushed for harbourmen, grackles and ganders squashed for villagers, songbirds squeezed for smart and silly maids alike. Every last remnant of those folks' feathered questions she'd wrung out, conserved, and dropped into the draught.

A bold combination, she had imagined, *for a bold lass. A stew to snuff doubts, to soothe and to succour, to sew up a split self.*

A month later, the batch is more bog than brew but still gurgling, its steam slicking the shack's soot-stained wall. 'Just about ready,' Winni says for the thirty-oddth time, but still the pot's waterline rises. Still the stew goes unsupped. Another flank of driftwood goes on the fire. Another swirl of the spoon. 'It's only missing one thing.'

Jinx *crrrrks* atop her shelf. Busy nitting and natting under her wings, she plucks a flurry of black down, offers no further comment. Winni admires the deft dartings of her head. The sleek scrapings of her beak. The blue bristlings of her proud breast. So efficient, so assured in her movements. So secure in her existence.

'What else can I do?' Winni asks, staring into the pot, stirring, stirring. All those brittle bones. All those everyday woes, those trivial worries. All those folks she's helped, all those times. *Try, Mither. Just try.* But then there's forever the one—'I don't want to hurt her, you know?'—the one she got so horribly wrong.

'If she only understood—'

Jinx's talons *scritch* against timber as she edges away to preen in peace.

'If I'd only told her—'

Scritch, scritch.

Stir, stir.

Outside, the tempest takes a breath. In the lull between howls, Winnifletch hears a familiar crunching on the path leading up to her door. The tread is heavy and irregular, a cautious scuffling. Like the tides, it draws close then recedes, rolls forth again only to stumble away. Her pulse two-stepping, Winni raps her long wooden spoon against the pot's rim. Clears it of sinew and scum. Holds her breath. The spoon raps again, its stem and scoop already clean, and again. Eyes down, she watches the grain fade as it dries. She won't peer through the window. She won't turn around. Only waits for the door to open behind her. For Shale to come in, drop her satchel and slicker on the water-stained floor. To toe off her boots, slide them under her narrow bed. No forgiveness begged and none offered. No change of heart or mind, not yet.

If only, Winnifletch thinks, afraid she'll never be able to spin the drift in Shale's direction, never rein it or her in, never rebuild her girl's outsides to match what's trapped in her deepest core. Afraid it's too late to for this spoiled sevenday spell of sorrow. Too late for her to fix anything. Too late to try again.

'Knock knock,' the wrong voice gruffs as the wrong person blunders in with the wind. The door whips free of his whiskey-slick grip, slams into shelves full-rattling with jars. Parchments whisk off tables and nightstands, garlands jangle, flames gutter in hurricane lamps. Startled, Jinx swoops through the chaos. With a flap and a flutter, she lands on Winni's shoulder, claws gouging. On the stove, the pot belches—and with a chortled curse, Wilke Maggaw does likewise.

'Get on in here,' Winni says, sharp as a sturgeon's snout. As he wrestles with the door, she peers around Wilke's cable-knit bulk, taking in the bare path behind him, the wide coast and frothing sea, the smudge of Lundey Isle in the distance.

'That's some hollow-blown gale,' Wilke says, lifting a longneck to his gob. Lipping for last drops. From the fumes reeking off him, Winnifletch guesses he drained those dregs more than once, hours ago. 'Reeled these feet of mine right off course for a while,' he says, 'right off course, those winds almost wobbling us anyway and anywhere but down here to Spinster's Cove.'

'Hm.' Winni squints out into the gloaming, looking far and near.

No glint of firelight in the Lundey's dark caves. No hint of warmth for the harpies nesting there. No torches bobbing up the evening blue strand, guiding young wanderers home.

'Could've waited until tomorrow,' she says, shouldering him in and the door shut. 'I'm going nowhere.'

'Ah, bluster.' To stifle hiccups, Wilke jams a fist against his chapped mouth. From a boiled leather sack slung low on his belt, he manhandles a limp-necked puffin. Holds the dead thing out like a tussie-mussie. 'Netted this beaut just for you, lass. Can't let it go to waste.'

Winni suppresses a sneer. As if he's doing her a favour, showing up like this, week after week, year after year, bag and guts a-swill with spoiled juice. As if the slop from any old corpse could heal his reef-raw skin. As if he's never learned a thing from her, not a single thing, to help himself. As if she doesn't have her own spells to squeeze. Her own baits to bottle. Her own perfect birds to break and remake.

The puffin was barely a fledgling, fragile as happiness in her hand. It won't be good for much. 'Sit,' she says.

'These legs will hold, Winnifletch. Better view from up here, anyhow, watching you work and such.' The red spidering on Wilke's nose and cheeks disappears, his face suddenly a single shade of fluster. 'Always were a handsome woman, Win...'

'An ounce'll do you for now,' she says, vise squealing, skeleton snapping, her own jelly jar collecting the creature's small drippings. 'Sip it slow and careful, right? If you want it to last.'

Old Wilke keeps talking as though she hasn't. Typical harbourman: tongue-tied 'til a dram or ten slippens his knots. 'Never could get my head around that Bear Ingersen's treating you so poor,' he says. 'A woman with your talents.'

A pause as Winni's head whips up, vision blurring. 'What's that now?'

'Leaving you holding the bassinet like that,' Wilke goes on, 'taking no care for his own pretty bairn.' Frowning, he swigs at his dry flask. 'Saw her up the strand, just now,' he says, quick-changing subjects the way only delusionals and drunks can. 'Your Shale. Keeping odd company, you ask me, strutting around in this weather with those hideous half-feathered lasses.'

'Oh,' Winnifletch whispers. 'Was she all right?'

'What an age we're living in, lass. Birds for best friends, Bear for a father.' Wilke turns and spits. 'Some Bear. *Hound*, more like, siring pups at every port, boasting about it between pints. Always, some sweetheart swallows the bilge water he's pumping Guess you've heard about his latest doings with Abe Mews' sweet Gertie? Bold-faced knocking on her boathouse window while the Stagg b'ys is away. Leaving his pawprints all over the place.'

Stupid girl, Winni thinks, numb from tongue to toes. *So stupid. But how?*

'Hoodwinked, she was. Same as the rest.' Swaying now, Wilke sweeps his rough hand around, taking in the workbench and stove, the iron pot and its month-long mouldering, the basket of broken bones on the table. 'What a cruel trick, shaming you girls into solitude.' He staggers forward and swipes the puffin juice from Winni's cold fingers. 'Playing you like that, then playing brain-dead. As if this beak-and-brinkle brew of yours has ever done more than wet a man's whistle.'

He lifts the jar with a chuckle, glugs it dry, then coughs himself even redder, words slupping from his whiskey-thick gob. 'As if it's actual *magic*.'

The puffin lies in the sink, untouched, deflated. Good for nothing even before that fool Wilke wrecked it—too gaudy, those tiny fluffers, more show than substance—but she'll save its meat for their supper. As ever.

Must get lonely out here, he'd said. Bear first. Then Wilke Maggaw. *A soul must get hungry for company...*

Winni grimaces. Still on her shoulder, Jinx stretches her neck and rawks. A long, low, chastising cackle.

Stupid, so stupid.

'Spells and spirits don't mix,' she says, hands trembling as she wipes down the vise. *That's* why the juice was weak tonight. That's why there was no change in Wilke's complexion, though he'd swilled every last drop. That's why the chafe hadn't uncracked from his cheeks. The old oaf was too drunk to absorb it. Too soused to see what she'd done, what she's *always* done, for him. For all of them.

'*Actual* magic.' She shakes her head. 'As if there's any other kind.'

All those years ago, her spell *had* worked, in unexpected ways, perhaps, but no less effective for all that. It hadn't hurt him, thank the stars, but it *had* done what she'd asked of it. Not as she'd wanted, of course, but even so. Though Bear hadn't stayed here with her, *something* kept drawing him back to Barradoon, again and again. His life *was* full of riches now, wasn't it? And in his own hound-dog way, he'd found bliss.

Actual magic.

Hopping from foot to foot, Jinx knocks her skull against Winni's. *Focus. Think of eagles, kites, jackdaws. Petrels and pelicans. Robins, sparrows, geese.* Proud migrators, fierce hunters—great wedges of birds that travel so far, so free, but only for so long and no longer. Mermaids of the sky, that's what Shale is, what she'll be. Sailing off into the blue each season, living, loving, then rewinging her course right back to where it, and she, began.

The right bird will bring Shale home.

The right brew will send her off again, broken, rebuilt.

Will it work?

Will it fix me?

A pause only Winnifletch notices, a twinge in her guts that says her instincts are good.

Risk it.

Faster than second-guesses, she snatches a fishing net off the floor, whips it around her shoulders, and traps Jinx in its tangles. *Think of falcon oil, fast-fixing the future. Think of eagle sap, true as north-star navigation, unerring in cast and course.* 'I'm sorry,' she manages, breath short and chest cramping as she slams the bundle onto the workbench, securing her grip as it wriggles. 'I'm so sorry.'

Think of this crow.

Think of Shale.

Together.

'Call her back,' Winnifletch cries, shunting Jinx into the vise, *twisting*. One, two, three turns, sharp and sure and *so sorry so sorry so sorry*. 'She'll listen if you call.'

My poor sisters, Mither.

This time the juice is good. It has to be. The flow is fast, the glass soon brimming. Hard to see through her tears, but she feels its strength as it trickles through her, the potency of Jinx's lifeblood. Bruise-black as the plumage Shale loved so much, dark but translucent, still as a moonlit night. A potion of perfect clarity.

Will it work?

Winnifletch is certain.

It's safe, she tells herself. *This drift will spin the right way. Our way. Here. Home.*

When the crow is dry, she lifts the body and cradles it close. *Bear was never broken. I've hurt nobody.* She presses a cheek against Jinx's cooling breast. Kisses her silent beak. Lays her quietly on the rickety stool. *Except my girls.*

'It's good,' she says, putting the juice on the workbench. Gently sliding the glass away from the edge. While she waits—she won't make Old Wilke's mistake; she'll not guzzle this pressing before its magic has settled; like a good stout, it needs to rest before drinking—she turns to the stove. Strains the bones from the stock, sixteen years and thirty-odd days too long in the stewing, then deposits them one by one on the table. Back and forth between cooktop and board, she collects and carries, splashes and spills. Eyeing the crow-glass. Sifting time for the right moment. Stirring for rifts to repair.

She lines up the longest shafts, fanning some into powerful curves, and pictures wings springing from Shale's arms, fitting and fletching her span. *Think of sinew and song and sleek silhouettes,* she tells herself, *think Sparrow and Starling and Soars o'er Stars.*

Hours pass as she puzzles the pieces together. Night winds hush into dawn. The sea shushes up to the shack's pilings, sighs slowly back. Soft light spills over the windowsill, yellow and rose, gilding the harpy's new frame.

Sore and sorry, Winnifletch finally gathers the glass. Jinx's juice. Shale's summoning. With eyes closed, she casts her mind over the water.

Think of the Lundey. Outside a murrelet cries, its *keer-keer* clear and cold. *Think of Henny.*

'Come back,' she says before sipping, slowly, steadily, the only spell she's ever swallowed herself. *Think of Leda and Crows-at-the-Sun.* The afterbrew burns, bitter and brutal. It whirls the churn in her belly, threatens to bring up everything she's ever kept down.

Actual magic.

'Come back,' Winnifletch whispers, deep in the drift, spinning. Limbs shaking, she fumbles for a chair, pulls it over to the door, close as she can without blocking it, and sits. Dizzy, she leans forward. Listens for footsteps, for Shale's sweet singing. Gulls wail as they wing overhead, away.

'Come back, my girl, and fly.'

WATERSLEEVES

'Uncle Fal took me to the after-dark yesternight,' Solen tells the great mound beneath her. It's an eight-foot drop to the beach over the grit-and-grass hill's blunt seaward face, yet the leap down's nothing to her. Just shy of six feet herself, Solen's landed it hundreds of times; but this raw morning she's flat on her belly, snaking closer and closer to the verge. Bony hips, ribs, elbows and knees grinding into damp sand. Too much cheap rum still a-throbbing in her skull. Eyes and cheeks smudged with last night's paint. Oilskin bag turtle-shelled on her back. For once, the air is tranquil up here, no wind whipping her uneven hair around or scouring her ruddy cheeks. clinging to salt-crisp tufts, Solen leans further forward and pitches her voice clear into the cave's maw below.

'I wanted to wait—I really did—but Fallon kept saying stuff like, *Cap Magaw's got her own schedule to keep* and *she's shipping southways before summer's end and taking the dolls back on the whaleroad with her* —and with limited space for seating amidship *The Rambler* and all, it's a *first come, first served* sort of deal for spectators... And when Fal said *it's now or never* on his way down to the docks at sundown, and *they're casting off day after tomorrow, you know*... well, that pretty much clinched it. I had to go with him. I *had* to see the show, Grizz. *Really.*'

A nose-wrinkling stench wafts up from the dank cavern sunk in the dunes. Vinegar. Sour gooseberries. Blackberry wine. Solen takes a stomach-settling breath and squints out at the small horseshoe cove before her. The spruce and pine woods scraggling the bluffs around Grizz's oasis. The ever-low clouds and restless grey water hemming everything in.

'Those dolls are *unreal*,' she powers on, sure he's at least half-listening now. Stinking in upset, maybe, but listening.

It's a start.

'I swear they're magic,' she says, 'though of course Uncle Fal denies it. *Smoke and mirrors*, he tells me, *that's all*, but I don't buy it. That performance was no trick of the light, Grizz. No magic lantern projection or shadow-play. Nuh-uh.'

The crag shifts under her weight and starts to crumble. Local gulls cackle overhead, smug wings spread wide as they surf the westerlies, tauntingly buoyant as Solen scrambles back from the collapsing edge. A lemon wave of curiosity reeks out of the cave, *sharp* but not strong enough to carry her friend along with it. At a safe distance, she splays out on the grass again. Rests her chin on her hands. Ignores the arsehole birds. Speaks to the version of Grizz she misses most.

'Somewhere, somehow, Captain Janny found two life-sizers—two! —and set them to singing and storytelling together—like, at the same time!—without anyone pulling the strings. Honestly man, there were no clever wires or fishing lines or anything hanging the dolls from the rigging. No castelet set up on deck to hide their masterful puppeteers. Nope, the two of them just came through this red velvet curtain Janny'd draped on the *Rambler's* yardarm, then started *walking* through the crowd like actual people, smooth as swans on still water, not clanking on little tin wheels like Tundish's ugly yuletide figurines.'

Now the citrus dissipates. The bitter fug subsides. Good, Solen thinks—the lad often forgets himself when a tale sinks its hooks into him—so she keeps going, lively as her churning guts will allow.

'No needle-wife in the isles has the skill to stitch such things together. There's no leather so supple, no fabric so flexible as whatever went into their makings.' She pauses, sniffs. 'Otherworldly, right? Had to be. Before they got going, they chatted to us in two or three different languages—ours, of course, and some other lilting tone-twinkles that human tongues aren't built for—kind of like chickadees calling, kind of like sleighbells, except, somehow, sounded out with words.'

Spoiled blueberry jam cuts through the gentle breeze now coasting in off the water. Yellow cheese veined with mould.

Dammit, Solen thinks. Propping up on her elbows, she cranes forward. Waits for the tang to mellow. Changes tack.

'Not gonna lie, Grizz. The more I watched, the more those dolls fluttered my insides. They're so tall, so graceful, so *perfect*. Neither lad nor lass, but somehow both, or neither, or something atween... Breathtaking even when they were goofing around. Pure *eleganza*— from the glim of their wigs to the shimmer on their mugs—they're chiselled and primped and painted to the high heavens. Lord only knows what makeup they use—crushed abalone? pearl paste? stardust? —but I want me some of that pale sparkle, like, *yesterday*. And when they danced...'

Solen sighs dramatically, camping it up for Grizz's sake. Real heat stirs in her belly, pinks her neck and ears. No act about it. 'How did they move like that? Without any flutes or bodhráns or fiddles sawing them to-and-fro across the deck? They swirled with their own strange tunes— like, music *unrolled* from the pastel silks dripping from their impossible, flexible limbs. Liquid songs spilled down their legs, each twirl somehow slick *and* swishing *and* chimeful... And then they did this *flourish* thing with their arms, and it sounded like waterfalls strumming a harp—and suddenly their long sleeves unfurled like birthday streamers, flowing right over our heads, and then *snap!* those watersleeves recoiled—'

'Okay, Len,' Grizz barks from below. Raspberry sorbet nips at her nose. 'I got it. They were beautiful. Now are you coming down, or what?'

Grizz's den is always dim. Tallowsticks glow in limestone nooks, flames low and forever guttering. A single oil lamp seethes orange against the sloped wall. Canvas tarps carpet the cavern's deepest shelter, no more than a few yards back from the flotsam littering its arched entrance, but the cold and wet aren't so easily squashed. Sog and sand stick to everything. Groundwater trickles down from the shell-stuccoed ceiling, a steady patter on the kegs Grizz has shunted to one side, a slow drip on his empty milk crates and book stacks, a startling plink-plink on Solen's stooped head. Great globs of his low spirit squelch underfoot.

The fug's thick in here, ever-changing but too heavy even for the sea to blow clean. Green apples crushed in a cider press. Mothballed linens in a widow's cupboard. Worms writhing on the footpath after a storm.

You should go home, Solen thinks hard at the mess of old patchwork cocooning her friend. He's burrowed right in, broad back turned and covers hooding him. A tattered wildflower garland lies tossed-and-turned to pieces under his rump. You should get changed. You'll get sick.

'Shove over,' she says, shaking rancid guck off her boots before kicking them off and squishing into the makeshift bed beside him. The blankets are clammy, clotted with eye-watering goop—a mix of skunk-blossom and blue spruce the now—but Solen finds the comfiest patch she can. Breathing through her mouth, she peels off her cable-knit crewneck and cargoes, strips down to her boxers and pit-stained undershirt. Nestling into the crook of his legs, she rummages through her bag.

'Did I mention their shoes? Heels like six-inch rivets, and the *shine* on them was something else!' She chuckles at the vision of Captain Janny wincing with the dolls' every step and not-so-subtly eyeballing the deck for divots. 'Not just glittery leather either, but—I don't know. Eel skin or something slick like that? And big enough to fit even my canoes!' She waggles her feet under the covers. 'Just imagine *me* strutting in a pair of those stilts!'

Encouraged by his muffled snort, Solen keeps yammering. 'You hungry? I got some leftover borscht in here—sweetest beets you've ever tasted and I stirred in a good spoonful Ril's own sour cream.'

Withdrawing an insulated flask, she gives him a minute before unscrewing the lid. Still warm, the soup's rich aroma cuts through the pong. Dill, beef broth, tomato.

'Go on, then,' he says, rolling over.

The quilts drape like motley robes around his bare bulk as Grizz grunts upright. Solen's lips quirk as she fills a tin cup to the brim. No doubt about it, he's still the burliest, hairiest bastard she's ever seen—they blunted four of Uncle Ril's razors once, scraping off that tangled beard of his, then pissed theirselves laughing at how wonky he looked without it—but he's still delicate for all that. Always has been.

Folk talk about old souls and kind souls and dark souls, but even with his deep thoughts and light tastes and oh-so-gentle touch, Grizz doesn't quite fit those catch-alls. Sometimes Solen thinks he's got a honeycomb inside him, buzzing with sweetness. Most times, though, she sees how his blues swell. How they coagulate. How they get too fulsome to keep in. Without warning, his foul mood gels out from under his soft chins. It slurps from his generous curves and folds. Wobbles like rose-sugar mallow as it blurps out in irregular blobs—some small and round as roe, others misshapen hearts as big as her fist—rubbery gobbets that she scoops into a pail whenever she can. No need for anyone to stew in that shit.

Now, while he's staining his muzzle with beet soup, she buckets a bunch of the stuff. Dumps three loads into the near-full barrels, leaves the rest where it is. Useless busywork, really—there will always be more —but it gives Grizz a bit of space. A bit of freshness.

'Maroon looks good on you,' Solen says truthfully—he's definitely an autumn, despite his love of corals—and the compliment slows the bluish ooze for a moment. 'Got some salmon to go with the soup,' she says, 'if you fancy it.'

Once again, she grabs her pack and wriggles in beside him, her own innards a-growling now the rum-poisoning's eased some. Grizz comes from a long line of Bonnebay fishers—folk say his kin settled these isles, staking their claim with hook, line, and sinker—and nothing tickles his palate quite like a prime marbled fillet or three. Uncooked, preferably. Fresh and raw as the sea that spawned it.

He shakes his head. Navy jelly dribbles from the dip in his navel, dark pearls of aniseed woe catching in his dark brown belly fur. His lips are slick with borscht and whiskers dripping, but the cup's just idling there in his paws. Almost full.

'Thanks, Len,' he rumbles. 'Save me some?'

'Suit yourself.' Solen peels back the foil wrapping, tucks into the fish with her fingers. Between bites, she sighs and smacks and chortles deep in her throat. *Waste not, want not,* Fal and Ril can't resist saying whenever she parcels another ten-pounder to bring down here, but her uncles can't fix Grizz with platitudes. There's no *fixing* what isn't broken. He's not wasting or wanting any more or less than she is. Than they all are.

So she eats in his company as always, and she sets fatty morsels aside for him, and more often than not she'll soon sniff them out again—hardly nibbled, wholly forgotten, and stinking worse than his temper. Later, while he's snoring through his lethargy, she'll scrounge up every gross ignored chunk, maggots and all, and toss it out to the breakwater before he wakes.

No big deal.

No need to make a fuss.

'Maybe they're wood,' Solen says, wiping the grease off her hands. 'Enchanted, obviously. No ordinary cooper could've turned their graceful pegs so seamlessly. Still and all, when they whirled past, sleeves snapping and undulating like the Otter Chute rapids, their perfume—or lotion or wig powder or whatever—smelled like that carved chest your Mither's got in the parlour. Cedar or camphor with a fuzz of green felt.'

She stifles a burp, swallows hard, hoping she hasn't overdone it with this morning-after glut. All good, she tells herself after a moment, then slips what's left of the salmon onto a crate next to a dog-eared novel. Resting on her haunches, she reaches over and gives Grizz a playful shove.

'Or *maybe*,' she says, punctuating each word with quick nudges, 'it was cinnamon! Ginger! Nutmeg! *Maybe* the young strangers baked them in their secret underhill ovens.'

That conjured a genuine smile.

Grizz is a dab hand in the kitchen when the mood strikes. Good enough, even, to go cook on the mainland, study under one of those stiff-hat chefs, maybe run his own bakery or supper-house someday—and Solen could go with him! Ditch her trawler and fishing-weeds and become his manager! His maître d'! His mainland matey!—but *who needs another public pig trough*, he'll inevitably say when she suggests it, or *things won't taste the same over there*, or *set menus aren't for me, Len. The best recipes are always spontaneous.* No use arguing, Solen well knows, so she just rolls her eyes, calls him an eejit, then tucks into whatever feast he sees fit to cater for folk over here. Trix's wake last winter. Harvest buffets for the Barasway Cup finals. And the bash he put on for Vera's farewell a few weeks ago—unlike her big brother, *she* couldn't wait to sail east to the big smoke, shake the cod-stink from her curls, climb mountains instead of masts for a while—and that shindig was nothing short of spectacular. After the crab cakes and lobster pie, the rollmops and dark rye, the bottomless bowls of chowder and loads of date crumbles, she and Grizz drank theirselves blind at a brandywine fountain, laughing and talking crap until one or both of them bawled.

And when—as ever—his squidge got a-rolling then, sad suet lumps jiggling down his candy-striped apron to splash in pungent puddles on his ma's kitchen tiles, Solen sobered enough to steer Grizz away from the grog. In a last-ditch stab at reviving his whimsy, she relieved the doorframe of a pretty garland they'd pegged up that afternoon, draped it like a leafy boa around his neck, then crowned him with a starfish and periwinkle wreath. *Prance, my queen! Prance!*

'If those babes *are* cookies,' she says now with a wink and a poke, 'then I'm ready for dessert.'

Grizz huffs a laugh.

'Tempted to check them out?' Solen teases—and for half a second, she imagines him nodding, saying *just gotta make myself purdy*, putting on a twang and a silly smirk that don't suit his regal snout, before he stretches off his weariness to stand so proud and tall that he breaks a hole clear through the rock, letting in the wan sunlight, howling with glee at the brightness of it all, hooting at the joy of being his big brawny self, his heart and legs thundering as he bolts naked into the water, where he splashes and belly-flops and scours away the past six months of sombreness until his pelt gleams and his beard is smooth as peach satin —but she knows his answer before the question's asked.

Already Grizz is scrubbing the grin off his face. Scooching down the rut he's worn into his blankets. Hauling those grotty old blankets back up.

For half a second, he smells like uncurdled cream.

'I'll catch them next time, Len,' he says through layers of cotton and wool. 'No doubt they'll come back soon enough.'

'Sure they will.' Solen smiles and pats his stout arm. Gives him space. Gathers her things to go. 'Sooner or later, they'll be back.'

SHRITHING SANDWARDS

Rowe finds the scattering of bones before any of the body's soft matter. A pelvis cracked open like a crab claw on the shore, scoured almost clean in the wash. Part of a ribcage half-buried a good ten feet away, gutless and be-gritted in the shallows, skeins of seaweed tangled in its prongs. Limbs piecemeal. A snapped thighbone staked through a ragged hank of denim, up where the wet sand turns to powder. Elbow joints akimbo in the dunes. Shoulder blades slicing dried clumps of kelp. Knees, still hitched to the shins, strewn in her path. Here and there, the shrill morning wind catches sinew filaments, sets them dancing all higgledy-pig. Ringless digits, cast like a far-seer's runes, tumble in the silt. A mostly meatless trail of carnage on the coastline.

Vertebrae blobbed with jelly-discs crop up all over the beach, some chunked with muscle, some tooth-scraped—but Rowe can't spot any pawprints around them, nor any sign of dog-walkers who might've loosed their hounds on this carrion. She frowns. It's too early for folk like them to be out a-strolling; this here's the undertakers' hour, not *theirs*. The sun's only just lipping the horizon; its wan yellow light skims the choppy sea to burnish dank divots here on land. Rowe crouches down by the water, traces hoof-crescents with her fingertip, brows pinched as she takes in the stampede of curved marks gouging the sand.

Standing, she rolls the legs of her coveralls even higher, slowly splashes towards Barradoon. Now dollops of flesh bob in and out with the waves. Pink paste scums the foam. She wades carefully. Keeps an eye out for the man's head.

That's often where real treasure lies. Gem-studded earrings, silver beard-beads, gold teeth. False eyes made of pearl and quartz and opaline glass. When corpses roll in with the tide—foreign sailors or mainland merchants whose ships come a cropper on Fortanach's Reef—most don't come with pockets stuffed, coin-purses bulging on belts, or a pirate's hoard of jewels twinkling on their sea-wrinkled forms. Most die unready, unadorned, wearing small wealth close to the skull. Most get dredged from the drink in one bloated blue piece.

Fat chance there's much worth hocking on *this* broken skelly-pile, Rowe thinks, trotting along the strand, but she won't let Garrup down by failing to look good and close. A fleet's worth of plunder couldn't repay his gruff kindnesses, but that won't stop her collecting every glint or sparkle that might bring some shine to his day. It's the least a gold-grubber like Rowe can do for a man with no blood reason to love her. And he does love her. Her Da. Garrup's never once shamed her for packing her skull full of whimsy; for play-acting Wealla the warrior as she scoops floaters from the shoals; for pretending she's Ingardena, the isle's first and fiercest mermaid, whenever his sons get too foul to bear as her own self. He's never hated her for being a foundling. A strange creature he fished from a tidepool. A thing who often wakes screaming, snorting, stomping like a stallion, and so sleeps in the byre like the beast she is. Garrup takes her as he found her. No more, no less.

While he's laid up with the gout and the b'ys—let's face it—are a pack of drunk fucks, it's up to young Rowe to rise before dawn. To reel in the family coin.

So she gets up. She goes.

shrithing sandwards
   salt and seawards
   bluehourshrouding

mantrotstalking
slinking
thinking
there
nayyyhhhrrrr
theretherethere
there he is
the liehole
the poke-and-prodder
the nightsnack
nayyyhhhrrrr
the
skinsnap
the
scaredscreamer
the
runcrunched
shinstomped
boar

Splashing past globs and gobbets, Rowe ponders what got this poor sod. If Marl and Castor were here instead of back in their bunks snoring off a cask of black rum, they'd start spouting shit about vicious mer-lasses out hunting these waters, those thick-thighed finners with sharks' teeth in sweet lady faces and a white pointer's appetite for blood. They'd swear up and down t'have seen those maids in action, bashing and biting some old capsized mate of theirs 'til he was nothing but chum and gnawed bone. Much like *this* mess here. Rowe pokes at the human sludge with a length of whittled driftwood, sure in her gut that her brothers are wrong. She's never once seen a seaborne mermaid, though rich folk claim to dine on their fillets. Those girls are just figments of men's fancies. Scapegoats for their own misdeeds.

Even Allton thinks they're made up. *Erl wasn't gobbled,* he'd say when the other b'ys got to yammering. He's the eldest—Allton's got

five years on Marl and Rankin, seven on Castor and ten on Rowe herself
—so if any Orr lad knows what's what, it's him. *Erl musta topped hisself
when Odessa left him. Cannon-balled into a riptide and didn't swim out.
No mystery there. No mermaids.*

But what else could've done such a number on *this* guy?

Rowe skips further into the water to wash the fatty muck off her
trousers. Sun's nearly full-up now; the bright's bleached the shallows clear
down to the seabed. Time to cut her losses, she thinks, maybe head on
over to the wharves to barter for some bread. Maybe dig up some cockles
or something. She can't go home empty-handed. Salt air whips her braids
and sets her long nose a-streaming as she scrubs from shin to chest with a
scrunched fistful of weeds. She shuts her eyes, dunks under. It's not that
Rowe's squeamish—she's seen worse gore than this up close—but a good
swim always gets her head back on straight. It gives her soul a good polish.

She guppies under the waves for a spell, peace bubbling past her for
a kick or two, until she strokes into a tangled mass of black hair. With a
jerk, she sputters to her feet. The man's head—what's left of it—spreads
like algae across the surface, bits and bobs clinging to the flotilla of his
beard and dreadlocked curls. The neck's a wriggle of shredded skin and
spine. The face is pulped, but the forehead's inked with symbols Rowe
knows by heart. The earflap glistens with studs of onyx and jet.
Heirlooms that left a stinging gash in her cheek last night in the byre,
when Allton—

Stop.

Her brother never takes those gaudy things off. Rowe can still feel
them scratching, his rough jaw a-bristling against hers, the gagging
stench of his breath as he huffed atop her—

Stop

—as she shoved and punched and writhed. Oh, he'd been deep in
the sauce, Kelloway's blackest black rum, but that was nothing new, his
best friend's a bottomless bottle, and he'd guzzled plenty more without
suffering the chill of his own lonely bunk, without seeking *her* out for a
warming—

Stop it.

No good ever comes from over-mulling things.

Just stop.

Count your blessings.

Don't think.

In her bib-pocket she's got two sand dollars for luck: one snapped, sure, but one's whole. Her coveralls are buckled tight at her hips and shoulders. Underneath, the knee-length pantaloons are still intact. That's got to mean something, right? The old granny gear Garrup gave her when she started undertaking with the b'ys—*For your protection, lass* —sure did the trick yesternight. Kept Allton at bay and her parts together. At least, she believes it did.

Sometimes, *believing* is the only option.

wrigglepig grapple
   in the
   wishswish water
   waveslaker
   ballbreaker
   slipslurpstruggle
   in the
   darkwetwhine
   stompstompstomp the
   dreadfeud pounder
   the
   wailhog slobbersnort
   stomp him into
   thighdust
   rumpsmudge
   skullsmush
   stomp until those
   pokeprodders
   shatter
   stomp until he
   stops

The Orrs were all born with sea legs—Rowe's are adopted, another gift from Garrup, along with her terrible pun of a name, but she swims like Ingardena, pure muscle and speed—so it makes no sense that the sodden pile of mash in the water is Allton. She rips off the bejewelled ear, stuffs it into her pocket with the seashells. Evidence for Da. For the b'ys. For the baileys.

There's no way Allton drowned.

No way he wasn't slaughtered.

She's heard talk about such crimes on the mainland, atrocities that happen daily *over there*, but not here on this old rock. Folk doing the unspeakable to themselves. To others.

Not here.

'What is this,' Marl says, burping foulness, when Rowe gets in and shows her brothers the ear. 'Some kind of sick prank?'

'No—'

'You're one twisted filly,' Rankin mutters into his prairie oyster. He's hunched at the kitchen table with the others, slightly less green around the gills than his twin but worse off than Castor, who's shovelling peppered hash and eggs into his gob like there's no tomorrow.

'What do you expect,' Castor says around mouthfuls, 'from some trickster's by-blow?'

Knock it off, Garrup calls from the bedroom, joints paining him too much to come and clobber the b'ys quiet like usual. Each word underscored with a thunk of the old sledgehammer shaft he keeps close at hand and suffers as a walking stick. *Let her be!*

'Thought maybe we should call the bailey,' Rowe says, hoping to out-talk their snide—

'Hear that, lads? The fiend *thinks*!' Rankin clunks the butt of his glass on the plywood board then downs the salted yolk and hot vinegar with a shudder. He grunts, slides sideways off the bench, then stands to free a long leather apron from its hook by the back door. Out in the fenced yard, the smithy's a-calling. There's rivets to forge, bowsprits to brace, wreckage to be reduced to iron ore. 'And why should Martin Keen buy what yer selling, shadowkin? He was with us that night outside Kelloway's, recall? He seen that flaming minstrel Low-key Highsson squat in a ditch to birth you, ten years ago if it were a day. Even with a kegger under our belts, we all seen you slip-trip from that ladyman's nethers, an inkish monster trip-trotting away like the nightmare you are, faster even than the chargers we was a-riding.'

'What a crock,' Rowe says with a click of her tongue. 'I'm at least fifteen already--'

'By whose accounting? Time moves different for young strangers like you.' Marl crams toast into his face. Chews. Retch-swallows. 'Who's to say Rowe won't be a hag by next week then a quivering colt again the month after?'

Castor snorts, replies to his plate. 'If she even lasts *that* long.'

Enough! Blankets rustle in the next room and bedsprings complain as Garrup shifts his great weight. He stifles a groan as his feet hit the dirt floor. *I mightn't have made her, but Rowe's our own lass just the same.*

Though she tries to snuff it, there's no tamping the joyful pink in her cheeks whenever Garrup barks at the b'ys like this. Putting them in their places and she in hers. *We're kin, you louts. Now lay off!*

Rowe grins as Rankin slams out the door and Marl hangdogs after him, bent on making it to the privy. True, their Ma isn't *her* Ma, that's clear as water—Credence Orr went groundwards yonks before Rowe came along—and the gods only know who sired her, but it sure as shit wasn't Low-key Highsson. The way Garrup tells it, she was a naked blue squaller when he found her in that rockpool—*Noggin bald as mine own, belly half again as round, barely bobbing above the tide. And Lord, what a gods-awful mouth!*—but he's treated her like his own since day one. He kept her when even her own mare wouldn't touch her.

When Rowe plays Wealla, Garrup is the shield offsetting her sword-arm.

When she's Ingardena, he's the twenty-gun sloop whooshing her off to war.

Lay off her, you hear?

Hush Da, she wants to chide as a sneer creases Castor's ugly mug. The lad gets up, shoeless in crinkled linen and leathers, and tosses his plate in the trough. An oil lamp swings over the table, wick burning low as his voice. 'Let's see this body of yours, then. Prove it's Allton, or—'

'It's him,' Rowe says evenly, despite her galloping pulse. 'Trust me.'

'Ha ha,' he replies, flat as a turbot. Refusing to meet her eye. 'I just dies at you, joker.'

all neigh for the
 mercymusher
 bone-twig basher
 malicemasher
 writhe worm
 all rear for the
 hogstiller
 bullbuster
 watch her
 stamp
 slay
 sate
 watch him
 writhe

'Tide must've took him,' Rowe whispers. 'Or maybe a beachcomber bagged him.'

It's a flimsy explanation and she knows it. This patch of coast is Orr territory; any and all wreckage is theirs alone to undertake. All bounty is theirs to salvage. No self-preserving 'comber would violate the filcher's code by sweeping this particular stretch of shore. And yet, somehow, it's been *swept*.

Nary a bone is mixed in with the sea wrack, not so much as a pinkie or toe. Rowe scuffs through reeking stacks of rockweed, squashing its eggish bladders, crunching periwinkle clusters underfoot. There's no hint of Allton in the dried brown clumps. No coils of black hair. No tar-stained teeth.

'I swear it was him—' Rowe begins, but now she's splatted like a squid on the strand, face-down with Castor's knee digging into her kidney, his callused paw grinding her cheek into the slurry. Waves lick at them both and slurp away. Rowe bucks and blubs, breath fizzing with salt. 'Get off—' She wriggles like kelp in a tempest, frothing and flailing, summoning her strongest Wealla spirit. 'Get—'

As she wails onto her back, Castor gouges her shoulders, her collar, her jaw, madly grabbing, holding, bearing down. Thumbs dig purple berries into her skin as he straddles her waist. Small fists hammer his lean thighs, thick arms, beer-ballooned gut. 'Get off!' Her skull pounds as he drives it down harder, harder. Leaning in close, he smothers her arms with his bulk. Growls into her ear.

'What's your game, filly?'

Rowe's nostrils flare. She sucks in his smoked herring breath, expels it with a grunt. Screws her eyes shut, looks inward.

I am Ingardena.

She takes another deep lungful, pushes it out.

I'm a warrior.

Each breath stokes the coals burning low in her belly, embers the b'ys have pissed on all her life. With this season's squalls spitting up little of worth, their moods have been more lemon than ever. Whenever five-moon storms like these ones strike, befouling seafarers and night-trawlers alike, ruddermen like the Orrs get trapped in the smithy for days, where they bellow and quench and clank songs for clear skies, making more bluster than goods. At tools-down, the stupid rain sends them to their well-worn booth at Kelloway's for more than a few tolls of the bell. Soon or late, always in their own time, they come a-swilling back home and a-sloshing into her byre.

First to gibe, to belittle, to degrade.

Then to test the snip of a wrench, the snick of a blade.

And last to shove their wrath into her—or to *try*.

Allton won't get a second fumble at Rowe.

I am Wealla.

And Castor won't get a first.

Fear me.

'Where is he, *filly*?' Castor asks, levering himself up a bit, pushing between her small breasts. There's a dull crack in Rowe's sternum. She gasps. Inhales fire.

Fury-wild now, she thrashes—once, twice—arching and levelling as her arms lengthen, strengthen, and encase in hideous armour. Castor bridges above her, unseated but steadily smacking Rowe numb as she snorts and neighs, tears streaming sandwards into her mane. Anger bubbles up her throat, a hot geyser of laughter, as she plunges a hoofish gauntlet into her pocket, her fingers hardening around the jagged shards of her luck. In a long, swift arc she swipes the sharp sand dollar out and up, slicing freckled flesh—hers? his? both? who knows? her vison's tunnelling, her slinkish legs stretching and stomping, her mouth widely whinnying as she slashes and splashes and—

shellslices
    jowljabs
    skullstaves
    hoofcracks
    chinsmacks
    knucklechaws
    stringmaws
    chewsprays
    gobstretches
    himhauls
    punishpays
    and

—then hears her horse-mouth shrieking in the marshes atop the Frillwater Flat.

Suddenly the afternoon sun's a used teabag dipping into the pekoe of evening. The seashore's now half a click away, down a fir-hackled slope petering into a low bluff, limestone bastions crumbling into that distant grey sand. Rowe's frozen but unshivering, shin-deep in the mire, not the beach, a harpoon-shot away from the Orrs' own backyard. No concept of how she got *here* from there. Pantlegs torn to pennants, skin scraped to shit, arms bashed like an All Hallows gourd. She feels none of it. Her mind's off a-flurrying in the wind, gusting in and out of a mermareish thing, a torment of inverted hoofs and scales and carrion teeth. A creature now capering in the rushes, now treading in Rowe's ruined boots. Top to tail, the beast is grimed with gore and red spatter. Its leathers and wools are full sodden. Its blue-black lips are chapped, howling.

Before it, Castor is nothing but a bunch of wet smears on its rough, canvas-clad hide.

A slop of butchery polluting the reeds.

She's numb to the shrinking of her strong forelegs, the loss of her bite and her brawn, her powerful kick, the shift from girl to ghoul and now into this—*what*—this something not quite herself—*what am I*— and something not quite other. It doesn't hurt, the darkling mare snapping and slurping back into someone Rowe-shaped. What hurts are the great black gaps in her memory when her brother must've sobbed for his soul. Her brothers.

Rowe roars.

The wind changes as she sloshes to the embankment, a thin cold stream carrying wisps of forge smoke and the upturned rasp of Garrup's shouting.

What in Rán's name is that racket? Marl? Sounds like a lamb's noosed herself in the fence. Rankin? Someone g'wan outside for a gander.

The girl inside Rowe cowers; her first instinct is to hide. There's cattails aplenty fringing the marshes and the water's a dinge of brown in the gloaming; she could hunker there with the red-winged blackbirds in among the tall stalks or else slip under the surface, ripple away with the brook trout. But, *I am Wealla. I'm Ingardena. I'm*— Something fiercer than the b'ys. A fighter.

A conqueror.

A killer.

Let them come, she thinks, yanking bundles of rushes out of the mud, tossing them onto the trampled raft of Castor's corpse. This new Rowe can handle Rankin—fat, radish-nosed hog of a man—and Marl's always been slower than molasses in winter. If she can just distract them, just cover the body awhile, just until she can give it a proper sea burial... Her palms blister and weep as she works. She's sweating by the time one of the lads comes huffing up the hill, but she's got a good rhythm going; it'll only take a few more fronds to make this disaster look natural, Rowe thinks, and between the twilit gloom and the fresh soaking she's had, there's small chance the fools'll glean the blood on her—

'What have you done, lass?'

The last stalk plips into the pond. It's not enough. Castor's curls still brillo above the blurline between water and sky. His banged up bare arm is unsunned, a buoy brightly bobbing to mark his hazard. One foot in and one out of the wet, Rowe stops. Lowers her chin. Slumps. Furls inwards. Yellow flickers from Garrup's lantern dance out ahead of her. Flames swimming with stars.

'What have you *done*?'

She can't turn around. Can't face him, her shield, her twenty-gun sloop. Not like this.

'I'm sorry, Da,' she whispers. 'I didn't mean—'

The first whistle and *crack* of Garrup's walking stick across Rowe's back staggers her; the second thrashes any hope of apology. She stumbles to a run. Skids on the grass. Skins her knees on hidden stones. Scampers upright. Pain throbs with each stride—spine, shins, heart—but she can't slow now, not even to steal a last glance at Da, to search for sympathy in his scowl, to say goodbye.

'How could you,' he calls, a croak in his voice that aches more than the lash of his cane. Now the sledgehammer shaft drops with a hollow wooden thud. Rowe hears his breath shudder, then he hisses '*Kin-killer!*' before hollering for her brothers. Rancour oils Garrup's awful joints and eases his hop-along step. He's a tugboat of a man, slow and stumpy but relentless when he's got the right fuel. This betrayal will keep him steaming for ages. He won't stop until she does.

Rowe knows there's no defending herself.

No forgiveness.

As she flees over the Flat, aiming nowhere but away from the Orr house, the smithy, the b'ys braying up the slope behind her, Rowe pictures Allton and Castor as they were *before*—hateful, hurtful brutes —she recalls the wicked weight of them atop her, the puke-prickle of their breath and bones, the gouge of straw and grate of sand, and she tries to summon that fey filly within—wilier than Wealla, more ruthless than Ingardena—she welcomes its blackening spirit, its wild willful harm, its obliterating hoofs. She invites it. Begs for its return.

Her thin legs tremble as she runs, weak things powered by fear, not fury. Over the fen to the limestone ridge, she scurries while the moon unmoors from the underworld and soars into the skittering clouds. In her wrecked boots, Rowe's feet are small and tender; the ground hardens as she goes, but she remains soft. Vulnerable. She is no mermare, no cantering revenge. Grass becomes forest becomes white-bouldered bluff. She sideslips down to the coast, knees jarring and ankles twisting as she misjudges distances, deep shadows taunting firmness in the silver-lit night. Crabs scuttle over the rocks, retreating to secret burrows in the sand. She follows, sliding on sea-scum, tripping. Splashing palms-first in a star-dappled tidepool. On all fours, she gulps in great chestfuls of salt air. Sweat and tears rain into the shallow water as she leans close, searching for limpets, barnacles, any wriggle of life in her silhouette. Wondering if, maybe, this was the puddle that spawned her. That would've drowned her, if not for Garrup.

Above, behind, the living b'ys bellow her name like a curse. She swallows a sob. Quakes upright. Tries to outrun the truth.

She's no Wealla. No Ingardena. No vengeful steed.

She's just Rowe.

Just a girl.

Alone.

REWILD

We won't speak their language. Our mouths and minds are too different —flesh can't converse with fae foliage, clumsy tongues with spry tendrils, mortal meat with enduring moss—but still we know them by heart, those blundering pale giants, our guests on these fortunate isles. Still we worry at them.

Their first sea-skimmers slooped into our natural harbours when we were much, *much* younger. Our whole colony was slow and scrubby back then, flocking bark and stone in shades of rust and chalk; not at all the fast-thallused creepers we are today, the clans of vibrant green speedy-spying as we roam. When they arrived, there were no hoof-and-wheel-scars yet crossing our bristling woods. No lean-tos or skin-sheds or smoke-puffing square houses braced on our mighty rocks. No hammers or hounds or hens ceaselessly clawing. No trees toppled and propped over restless grey waters, no little platforms to support the soft ones' stick-and-line jigging, no skinny traipseways to tether their boats. None of their silly toothpicks stuck in the ocean's great maw.

Nowadays, they relentlessly bore into the earth, white-anting our foundations, mining for fire-black and fresh water. They splinter birch, ash, alder—once our favourite abodes—before stacking and restacking them into cloud-scraping steeples, lighthouses, masts and maypoles.

Pine forests become logs become homes. Clay is baked into flame-boxes that bake loaves. Sand melts into mirrors, windows, brew glasses. Dirt mashes into footpaths and town squares, daubs wattle walls, barrows into burial mounds. Fat flocks nibble our natty heads, tickling us trim. Sometimes these woolly ones cleave too deep, sometimes they clad us in hanks of white fleece, but they always bleat before the axe falls. Sharp spade-songs reshape our horizons. Steam, steel and sails swift new life to this land, brusquely billowing out the old.

Oh, what imagination is stored in the boneballs a-wobbling on human shoulders!

What ambition is cooped in their friable chests!

What delights are yet stuck in their deepest insides.

Without us, the whole dreaming lot of them would be stifled. The lads in their eggshells. The tricksters in their caverns. The wives in their journey-chests, the husbands deep in their cups, the babies a-swill in salt water. The mermaids in charge of far-travelling fleets and those tangled in stink-sodden holds. The weather-workers and spell-spinners and otherways-walkers. The poor sods who seek out their strange secret fixes.

We were aimless before those first keels scraped onto our shores. Free and fearless, it's true, but also flailing for purpose. Meaning. Connection.

Now we are driven.

We are fond.

Protective.

Proud.

Shadow-silent, we watch and pry and help them thrive.

Down on the wharf our ochre-flaked kin steadily munch the silver-scale sellers out of their tiny timber booths. Along the coast, our liverwort sisters scallop boathouses and potting sheds and fog-feathered factories; spores spreading as they mush weatherboard walls and crack cobbles. Further inland, our sphagnum star-kin spangle hills and valleys, shifting soil and structure alike, creeping inside to unsmother the laced-and-buttoned softies trapped in timbered and tiled cages. From fen to fells, we quietly tend to our visitors. We rearrange their frail foundations. Their fates.

It is, we've realised, the least we can do.

Especially for folks like the ferocious stormers up on the Freshwater Flats! See how they lash and degrade each other? How they thrash and stomp and sozzle themselves? Hear their bellows squeakily slowing, their forge embers sizzling and sighing and snuffing right out? Feel the damp seeping into their smithy while they sneak off to the stable? Feel the splash as they scratch and smash and slash that little shapeshifter until she soaks our loam good and deep. Smell the rot.

Now, step back.

Watch us work.

Don't breathe a word—we certainly won't—as we moss up their smithy, lichen their house and privy and rickety byre. Don't ruin the surprise. The *reward*. Can you see how we're saving these men? Remaking them with our grappling and gnawing and good-natured goring? See how we're crackling, crumbling, crushing their cabin? Next —just you wait—we'll rewild them all, these furious lads. We'll unleash their inner beasts, let them *rove*.

No need to thank us, we'll think but never say. *Such raw power should not be contained.*

EBBTIDE

Aegis the Cackler told Winnifletch a story once, about a word-weaving witch from the mainland who picked a pouchful of stones for her final burden, an industrial riverbed for her grave. A drear tale from a rib-tickler like Aegis, Winni thinks as she wades in dawn-pinked shallows within sight of her hut, the cove's shingle cold as misery underfoot. Even now, she can't quite fathom why a popular witch would ever choose to rest in a forgettable city-slopped river, with nothing to speak for her but a pile of blank rocks.

Already Winni's up to her shins in the sea—she's always been attuned to its cadences, its clouds, its changeable tides—and her tanglesmithed cloak's glugging greedily, its double-knotted ties gouging into her neck, its worsted lengths dragging her into the deep. Her pockets bulge with precious keepsakes, not pebbles; memories to best weigh her down. A crystal phial a-swirl with red liquid. A clever raven's skull. A mermaid's silver-sheathed dagger. A baby girl's feather-flocked boots.

Little monuments folk will find on her after she's drowned.

Blue-toed and bleary, Winni faces her chosen fate, a spell-spinner thumbing charms no one wants anymore. Grasping for real magic. Water glugs around her numb calves, wicking up her grey linen skirts as she slowly swills forward. With each step, she casts her mind deeper into the drift—that elusive, fortune-filled aether forever taunting her—what some folk call *hexways* and others *witch-weather*, but most avoid naming at all.

True magic can't be pinned down, Winni knows, like some prize trout on a board, its lustre lost, size and scale labelled. It wanders where it will or nowhere at all. It flies free.

It takes more than cunning to tap into this source. More than an old witch's timeworn tricks and tools. More than her faith.

What it takes, Winnifletch thinks, is a soul in great need.

A soul who greatly needs *her*.

Gaze split, Winni watches the chop cresting out to the horizon ahead *and* the drift-smoke roiling all around her, its messages vague and meaningless. She sees her so-called power for what it is now, what it might always have been. Nothing. A mumbling, mutable fog.

She lurches into a foam-crested wave.

How long has it been since she last bubbled a sparrow-broth for Yarmouth Weaver, light cupfuls to keep that gran's thin fingers deft on the loom? How long since she's crushed balm out of cedar waxwings, pinkish passerine paste to soothe the cracks in Mere Tallon's ancient, net-knotting hands? How long since troubled lasses have come a-knocking on her door, bartering fresh bread or glass beads or heirloom tomatoes for Winni's enchantments? How long since she's hunched over her workbench for hours, crushing cormorant after albatross after strong Northern gannet, squashing hollow-boned corpses into potions? How long since she's distilled nectars to reverse double-crosses; tonics to suppress crib-coughs; tinctures to reel in wayward hearts; elixirs to tuck long-awaited bubs in their mithers' bellies or philtres to ease the unwanted ones out? How long since Winni's been so honoured—so *humbled*—to hold a woman's very happiness in her gnarled hands?

It's your body, she'd always told those most desperate lasses, no judgement, no shame, no regret. *Your choice.*

How long has it been since her own—only—daughter wailed for a fix of her own?

(Oh, how Shale had *begged* for the feathered frame Winni had finally crafted, too many years too late—*When's it my turn, Mam?*—

how she'd *pleaded* for a harpy's sleek shape to reflect her avian spirit. A winged cure for her deepest woe. *Why won't you help* me?)

How long has it been since Winnifletch really helped anyone?

How long since she's actually *mattered*?

Who knows, shushes the sensible sea. *Who even cares.*

A drear tale, Winni thinks even now, sloshing into her retirement.

Suddenly Winni's soaked up to the knees, stumbling forward, shivering from skull to sole. Despite herself, she snatches at the thick layers tugging and twirling around her, threatening to trip. The white-worked shift beneath a grey smock and kirtle, the oversized fisherman's sweater, the stained apron hanging halfway down her thighs, the hand-me-down cloak o'er-swaddling it all. Stupid, she knows, to wear so much—her toes are dead white already, her skin's prickling with goosebumps, her jaw's clenched against the rattle of teeth—stupid how pride *clings*. She doesn't mind folk poking and prodding, *after*, or pawing through her pockets, but she can't bear them finding her naked. Night-trawlers fishing her out of the drink at dusk or harpooning her bare corpse when it rolls in with the next tide. Their hooks slipping, at first, skimming across her private fullnesses and folds, before finally snagging their water-pruned catch. A bloated, slippery seal.

She's dressed for dignity, for *heft*, but still she yanks at her anchoring clothes, still she struggles against them. Huffing, she pauses. Turns to gauge how far she's come. Catches her breath before it's good and gone.

There's a five mile stretch between her cliffside shack and the bustling shipyards at Barradoon harbour, a wide curve of coastline skittered with blue crabs and clumped with stinking skeins of brown kelp. Soft dunes gently sift upslope where drunks and lovers sometimes lay their swooning heads, too pickled to make it to the bluff's rune-marked grotto, that acoustic mecca for guitar-strumming lads on wistful silver moon nights. Winni squints.

Frowns.

Strange to spot folk within hollering distance at this ungodly hour.

Out here, early mornings belong to the wretched and lonely.

But now there's a trio of b'ys silhouetted on the westward shore, four miles or so downwind, scraggly things wrangling a Jon-boat out of the wash. Quarrelling, from the looks of it. Their fists thrashing between pushes. Their petulant, full-body heaves.

Winni turns away, splashes on ahead. Sucks in sharply as the sea slaps up to her waist.

It's all yours, lads. You can have it.

She won't miss this place.

Not her breakwater hut on its twenty-foot stilts, its back wall bolstered by a sheer limestone crag. Not the timber jetty spindling out its opposite side, a platform and patio and promenade in one, balanced on barnacled pilings. She won't miss the small icehouse nestled under its salt-crusted belly, tucked in the crook where blunt cliff meets slick stone. Nor the iron ladder skulking down from a hatch in the kitchen floor. Nor the weatherworn steps leading no one to her front door.

Last night, Winni had said farewell to it all with brush and broom. She'd scrubbed the workbench's bird-spatter and blood and brew-stains, leaving nothing but ghosts in the whorls. She'd banked the fire, blacked the potbellied stove. Her ladder-back chair and a child-sized stool went back in their spots by the hearth. (How many times had Shale leapt off that little yellow seat, arms flapping, yearning to fly?) Blades, handsaws, nutcrackers and hammers went back on their shelves, alongside crab traps and cockle pails, crocks and clay pots, vials of seeds and shells, murk-filled bottles, rusty tins, candle stubs, quartz and flint. All the flotsam of her craft, her life. Her past.

Come daybreak, Winni half considered leaving a note for her daughter—but decided against it. Let her cold blue body speak for itself.

Hands now plunged in submerged pockets, she clutches the crystal vial, the skull, the tiny sodden boots. The sea is hungry this morning, eager to swallow its due.

Nearly there.

'Ever seen a flesh-eater up close? You know, those kelpish mer-lasses with their dagger-filled maws? Not the seafaring maids, gods love 'em, but the ones whose hip fillets are so damned expensive, only the top-hats up Ballyhack Hill ever supped on their fatty white flesh?'

The voice nearly bowls Winni over. Sloshing around, she scours the beach behind her, the hut up on its pilings, the sea-scummed breakwater underneath. There, just beyond the tideline, a bundle of leather scraps and wool rags hunkers on a big, trollish boulder. Chapped mouth chawing on words Winni can't always catch.

Shale?

Her breath snags—but that traitor hope soon scrapes back down her gullet. Winni blinks as the figure shifts into a lankier shape than her daughter ever bore. No wings on this lass, no feathers. Just dull brown braids scraggling over stooped shoulders. Dark eyes sunken and cheeks staved in. Coltish limbs furled in the pier's shadows.

'Saints and sinners, girl,' Winni hisses, palm pressed to her thundering chest. 'You near scared the soul out of me.'

'My brothers swore they hauled in a mer-lass once,' the skinny thing went on, lips split and red-crusted, sights fixed on drifts even Winni can't see. Sunlight glints on her lashes and snuffling nose as she eases herself closer to the stone's rounded edge. Trousers torn at both knees, bare arms purpled with bruises, fists crosshatched with cuts and scratches. 'But you know how b'ys are. Full of lies and vinegar, the lot of 'em. Lies and vinegar.'

'How long you been out here, child?' With a grunt, Winnifletch hitches her wet weeds, skirts slurping as she slogs shoreward against the waves. At last, soft sand firms into pebbles. Winni treads careful now, dead feet unsteady on her old stomping grounds. 'Where you from?'

The girl stiffens.

'Where's your kin?'

She scuttles back into the gloom.

Skittish as a sparrow, Winni thinks, slowly heel-toeing her way across the strand—but once she reaches the boulder and gently croons her down, the lass's icy grip is crushing.

Strength enough to spin a drift...

'Why didn't you knock instead of freezing out here?' Winnifletch asks the wee witch who's come to succeed her. 'Come on in, child. Let's get you warm.'

'The key goes here,' Winni says, jamming the short iron rod into a recess above the lintel. 'Your choice if you want to use it. Only locked the place up myself yesternight because—' *I wasn't coming back* '—I didn't know you'd be here so soon.' She gives the frame a quick pat, props the door open with a wooden wedge, then stands there dripping. Already smells stale in here, she thinks, with the cupboards relieved of perishable goods, the draughty gaps around the kitchen's trapdoor plugged with moss. Like the hut was holding onto its breath 'til someone new called it home.

'Opens the icehouse, too. Not too much down there the now—a few gannets I netted in that storm last week, maybe a couple guga, and a fine gentleman pelican. The lot should still be pliable enough for a philtre or three—the stiff won't have got deep into them yet. Anyways,' Winni says. 'I'll show you where 'tis before I go.'

May as well be talking to herself for all the girl replies. Winni can't pin her age—mid-teens? Early twenties? The creature's worn thin as a second-hand dishcloth, but she's got a strong face. Long nose, narrow chin. Equine, Winni's heard folk call it. The young witch frets around the room, fingertips brushing bedposts and blanket box, leather jesses slung on a driftwood roost in the corner, unstoppered bottles. Her gaze twitches here and there and back again, alighting most often on the lone shuttered window and cracked-open door. Fair light peters in with a fug-lifting breeze, the call of crows and rough beach-combing men, but sunshine and birdsong don't ease the hitch in the girl's shoulders. She creaks across the boards, never settling for more than a second. Lips endlessly spitting somethings Winni can't quite hear. Is she casting protections? Marking her territory? Laying her word-prints all over the place? Claiming the spindle-legged hut as her own?

Whatever drives her, the girl's roving sets an eel-wriggle in Winni's guts.

'If you're deft with gulls,' she continues, 'you'll have stock aplenty here. String a net above the jetty and you're laughing. If it's terns you're after, you'll have to trek further down Gallahorn way. The isles off Northman's Cove are lousy with puffins, mind, if you can bear to crush those sweet little dumplings.'

Hush now, Winni tells herself. Rambling like a ballyman at the solstice fair. Who's to say this new drift-spinner skews skywards anyway, just because she herself always has? What with the lass blathering about those pricey mermaids earlier, she might work water currents for all Winni knows. Maybe she squeezes spirit and spells from cod, halibut, deep-water carp. Maybe she's got a touch fine as fishbones. Maybe the poor souls come a-knocking on *her* door will expect brine, not birds, in their brews.

Hey hey! shouts a baritone snarker some ways down the strand. *Lookee here!*

The girl stops her scuttling, lifts her head to meet Winni's eye. Terror and defiance war on her face. Her voice comes out thick, trembling. 'You ever lost yourself to the cold? Like, you ever turned cold to the very core of your being? So cold your deepest self bursts right out your shape, then flies so far and fast you can't feel a thing your body's doing back down on land, empty and all on its own?'

'Kindling's over here,' Winni says, shaking her head as she crosses to the hearth, 'and there's sufficient birch and applewood in the undercroft to see you through the week. After that,'—*I'll be gone*—she gestures at the hatchet beside the chisels on her workbench, 'it's over to you.'

Enough's enough, Rowe!

Come out, come out...

The girl flinches.

'Ah,' Winni says as the b'ys bellow outside. She fetches a handful of sticks from the basket. Teepees them in the woodstove's ashless belly. Scrunches dry bark and seaweed, scrapes steel against flint. 'Rowe, is it?'

The lass nods as the tinder crackles.

'Some folk have a hard time letting go, don't they? When it's time to move on.'

Winni straightens, dusts off her hands. The fire's nice, she must admit. The sea's chill has got into her joints; if she lingers here much longer, she won't have the limber to get back down the stairs. Still, she tells herself, there's enough morning left to get a pot of starch on the hob. To have a care for this wee starveling.

'You're no driftspinner,' Winnifletch says at last and Rowe's frown confirms it. She's no witch, no hex-ways wanderer—just a lost, fuddled kid. A pearl shucked from its shell, thrown away. 'Never mind. Toss a log on, then come over here. Let's get some food in you and some salve on those scratches.'

Just like that, the stove's piping once more, a jar of molasses beans a-bubbling. The brew-kettle's warming, slow-melting beeswax with lavender oil. Shale's little stool is clunked down in its old grooves beside the worktable, Rowe perched on its flaking seat, quietly watching Winni thunking ingredients—mugwort, nettle leaf, goldenseal root—one by one, on the bench. Soon the pestle's grinding in a soapstone mortar. Honey-fat and herbs blending into cream. Old habits dying hard.

The blood stink's rank on ye, Rowe! We can whiff it all the way from here!

Show yourself!

Winni daubs Rowe's slashed knuckles, cleans red grime from coarse fingernails, overlooks the streaks of rust staining her coveralls and cuffs. The lass winces at the gentlest touch.

This way, Rankin. I got me a hunch!

Winnifletch quakes in her damp garb but keeps chatting like she'd only just met Rowe for pea soup and doughboys at Ma Clary's. No rush, says her tone. No worries. Even so, the girl's tense as a jackrabbit at the wood's edge, sniffing her options: to bolt or burrow in for good.

Go get the boat, Marl! No, bring it here, *ye dumb sod. Lord knows she won't come easy...*

'There, now,' Winni says. One last swipe and the sweet-smelling balm's rubbed in. Another log goes on the fire. Two for luck. Vapour wisps from her skirt and cloak as she passes Rowe a bowlful of hot stodge. Outside, the sea's song changes pitch as the noontide beckons, waves rushing out with a gravel-bass tune. 'That's my cue to go,' she says then, tidying her table for the last time. Again.

Rowe's spoon scrapes against enamel and clay. Even with a bellyful, the girl's a mess. But she'll get there, Winni thinks. She'll be fine. This hut's been a haven to women far worse off than her.

'Stay as long as you need,' Winni says, reknotting her cloak ties, checking her pockets. 'It's your choice.'

No flourish as she returns to the door, no farewell as she flings it wide. Winnifletch steps outside—and stops short on the landing.

A-ha!

Knew it!

She's in there, Da!

Less than a click away now, two lank-bearded lads and a bald man twice Rowe's age are a-stomping up the hard-packed silt at the waterline. Gutting knives strung on their belts. Blades bare in their fists. Black maws wide and yowling. *Ruddy kin-killer!* Beagles drunk on a hare's scent.

Blood for blood, lass!

Blood for blood!

'No,' Rowe says as Winnifletch retreats inside, locking up for the second time that day. 'It really isn't.'

'The b'ys out there,' Rowe whispers. 'My brothers— well, some of 'em anyway, there used to be more, but what happened to Allton and Castor, I didn't mean—'

'*Whssht*,' Winni stops her. Hand up, brow corrugating. 'I know, child. I believe it.'

Rowe isn't the first broken girl she's hosted under this roof, nor the first she's taken too long to read right.

(*When's it my turn, Mam? Why won't you help* me...)

As the men's barking grows louder, Winnifletch withdraws into the drift, studies the spirals swirling thick and fast in the fire-lit gloom. Hot rage rises from her belly, snagging her throat so fast she nearly chokes. Heat prickles up her neck, burns her right to the scalp. Sweating now, she focuses on Rowe, *really* looks at her. Shame lumps around the hook in her craw. Dread squirms in the pit of her gut. Disgrace.

What sort of driftspinner misses so many black signs? So many obvious sin-marks? Winni shakes her head. Is she really *that* out of touch? Has she ever really helped anyone?

Waves wash over the breakwater below, their froth and foam tongues hissing, calling her out to sea. On my way, she tells it. Soon.

But first, Winni observes the poor lass's own truths, flickering bright as a magic lantern-show in the drift's currents. *There*: baby Rowe soot-smudged, her soil-cloth leaking, a coal scuttle her only cradle. *There*: Rowe, a muck-featured tot, scrawling for scraps beneath a rough board, forks stabbing like lightning whenever she snatches a rind. *There*: a chorus of whinnies as older b'ys taunt three and five and eight-year-old Rowe, brothers all gallumphing around her, horsewhips stinging as they nicker, as they laugh and lash and corral her for kicks. *There*: in some sort of barn, Rowe bedded down with the lads' steeds, Rowe with no home in their house, Rowe a young woman now full-budded and moon-blooded, Rowe still scrawny but not so small she can disappear, no matter how tightly she balls herself, how silently she sinks into the straw. Rowe can't escape the extra weight that crinches and crunches atop her in the night, the flurry of callused paws grabbing, prodding, the hard things sticking in soft places they don't belong. *There*: Winni sees the great crimson flash of Rowe's breaking point. The moment not so long ago—no, the *moments*—she shed her bruised self and became something else. A tempest of teeth and fists and purloined blades. A one-woman stampede fiercely gnashing, pummelling, biting, stomping Allton first, then Castor, her worst offenders. *There*: Winni spies the bludgeoned mess she made of the b'ys. The horrible messes.

We got you now, girl!

'I can't go back out there,' Rowe says, quiet but firm. For once, her focus seems fixed in the here and now. Her eyes are clear as she glances 'round the kitchen, taking in the workbench and tools, the bits and bobs of a driftspinner's trade, the hard facts of her predicament. Chin lifted, she says, 'Not like *this*.'

For once, Winnifletch doesn't hesitate.

'Sit tight,' she says, fumbling the dagger from her cloak pocket as she hurries to the kitchen. 'Actually, get up. Take that clay pot—' she points the sheathe at a tripod rack in the corner, 'fill it with *that*—' points at a slurry-filled Mason jar on a ledge above the sink, 'then lid it and stuff the lot in the fire. Haul it out again the instant it starts whistling. Mitts are on the hook!'

Kneeling beside the trapdoor, Winni blades the dense moss clear from its edges, then flings up the hatch. A gust of fresh air brines the room, a powerful *whoosh* that sets Winni's eyes a-streaming. She grins, breathes deep—'Back in a tick!'—the ocean's roar matching the growl

in her chest. Down she goes, skirts tucked between her legs, hems
shoved in her apron's waistband, bare feet sliding on wet iron rungs.
The ladder is salt-rusted but sturdy, so cold it burns, but she streaks
down it, nimble as a lass half her age—though she's not *that* old, really,
maybe two score and five years, maybe less—she's otter-quick despite
the knife in her grip, the sea-swell in her joints, the crick in her hip she'd
planned to cast off today. At the cliff's base, she swoops into the
icehouse. Snatches supplies she'd shored up for Barradoon's next lonely
witch.

Water pitter-patters from the ceiling, metronome drips marking
time on the raw timber floor. Lungs heaving, Winni rejects half the
stock on her shelves. Rowe isn't Shale, she tells herself; this lass is no bird
at heart, no harpy disguised as a daughter. Not with that piebald skin of
hers, that wild mustang mug. She's an altogether different sort of beast.
Harmed, harrowed, haunted...

Hurry.

Winni wriggles a sandpiper into the makeshift pouch of her folded
skirts, but her every instinct knows this ingredient won't cut it. If this
spell's to work—*will it, though?* will *it work?*—the brew's got to be
ferocious. A force of salted earth and restless seas.

Exhaling, Winni lets her gut guide her, though it's let her down
before and may well do so again. (*Why won't you help* me?) Now she
seizes a horsehair sack full of cuttlebones. Rips a pair of seal flippers
down from the rafters, slips them into the bag. Snaps the fine pelican's
neck, stuffs its kinked carcass in with a snarl of shell-dotted kelp. She
bunches the bag's neck, noosing it with her cloak ties to keep her hands
free, and clambers up again. Ril's cure clunks against her spine. Hopes
rise.

Winni's done more with less in her time.

She has.

She *has*.

'It's piping!' Rowe shouts as Winni crests the hatch and dumps her
scroungings onto the kitchen floor. 'Haul it out,' she yells back, then

grunts herself all the way into the hut, latching the trapdoor while the girl's kin swear a blue streak half a mile long below.

Spots swim in Winni's vision. She takes a deep breath, bends to scoop up the sack, and when she straightens the drift is *everywhere*, thick as clam chowder. The curls and coils of possible futures shine like gold thread in the tumult, strands she can *almost* touch and tug and spin.

'What do I do?' Rowe asks, cheeks flushed from the fire, boiling pot pressed between quilted mitts.

We got you now, girl!

We got you!

'Work with me,' Winnifletch says, calm as the doldrums once she spies Rowe's essence in the drift, her true self, her best chance at escape. 'We can do this.'

We *can*.

Winni upends the bag onto her workbench while Rowe puts the pot down within reach. Together, they wrangle the pelican's head into the vise. The lass holds it steady while Winni turns the crank, chanting charms into its flesh. Soon the blades of its beak snap like hardtack. 'Shove these all the way up your sleeves,' she says, handing them over to Rowe, 'then rope 'em in place with *that*.' The lass does as told—*Shale was never so biddable*—sliding a slim shard under each of her cuffs then wrestling walrus-gut string around her wrists. While the girl struggles with sinew and knots, Winni wrings pelican skull-silver into the brew. Next she presses levity and speed from the sandpiper, pours this good juice into the mix, then adds four hanks of kelp. A wreath of plaited grass. A skipjack's dorsal fin and serrated tail. Without pause, she sings luck into the pot, channelling long years for Rowe and the widest horizons. A far-distant life worth living.

It'll work, she tells herself as the liquid browns, then burgundies, then blackens. She stirs and *stirs* as the drift glints with promises and the potion burbles like an innocent babe. Rowe has secured the bindings at last. Now she waits, rum-berry eyes wide, hands shielded and beak-sharp, for her next command.

Winni's mouth is too dry for talking.

This *has* to work, she thinks—but will it? Magic is fickle. It's *feral*. It flies where it will. Some days—Winni must believe this, she *must*—it responds to souls in great need. Today is just such a day, she tells herself, fossicking in her pockets for the small sacrifices that'll clinch it. The crystal phial, the raven's skull, the booties. Cherished relics of her past. Her heart's heaviest hoard.

Winni swallows.

Lets go.

This time it'll work.

'Your hair,' she says, chest burning as she uncorks the faceted bottle, pours in its red. Then she plinks in the skull—*poor Jinx*—and Shale's first pair of shoes before turning back to Rowe. 'Rip out a good handful, a whole braid if you can, and chuck it in quick. The pain will pass soon enough.' Again, the lass complies, wincing out a great greasy brown hank without tears or sass or second-guesses. Winni thanks the fates for small mercies. 'Wear this like a hood,' she says and tosses her the horsehair sack. As Rowe carefully manoeuvres it onto her head, Winni strains the draught into old Aegis's sturdiest firkin then cools it with a flourish of her fingers, a whirlpooled thought.

'Take this now,' she says, ladling a cupful of milky green broth and handing it over. 'Drink up.'

Thunder booms on the stairs outside. 'Nowhere to run, Rowe!' A hurricane batters the weatherboard hut, ham-fists and boots pounding for blood. 'Marl's on the 'neath ladder, so don't even try it. We got you now, kin-killer. We got you!'

'Mither, help me,' the girl whispers and Winni's knees jelly before she remembers—*I never gave Rowe my name*—that it's just an empty word. *Mither.* A go-to like *Ser* or *Hen* or *Pastor.* Mere politeness for a stranger. It doesn't mean anything.

'Stand on these,' Winni says, crouched at the girl's feet, lifting then plunking them squarely on the seal flippers. This'll work, she thinks, creaking upright. Focusing on Rowe—her long teeth and long chin, her jerry-rigged arms, her nervous wobble—she ignores the men's din outside, their cruel invective, the vicious abuse of her property, her *home*, and calls to mind a speech she'd prepared, years ago, a summoning for a different child's transformation. A different child's urgent need.

At last, she gets to recite it.

'Think fast and hard, lass,' she says, weaving the drift through each sound, each syllable, spinning strength through soul-aching sorrow. '*Be* the shape you imagine, the someone you most want to be. *Become* her in psyche and spirit. *Believe* you are her, deep in your innermost spark, and the body will follow.'

'Rowe!' Marl screeches through the floorboards, the hatch juddering against his blows. 'Open up!'

'Say your prayers, killer!' The front door jolts, handle jangling and planks creaking, as the other two hot-temper against it. 'Give her up, witch!'

'Never mind them,' Winni urges, furling Rowe in the billowing drift, gently nudging the cup mouthwards. 'They can't hurt you, not here, not anymore. Not if you concentrate, lass. Drink up now. Let's get you gone.'

Two gulps and Rowe's secret self starts to muscle its way out, her girl-form shedding, slinking away like smoke. Winni hums an old tune while she spins her spell, one of the Cackler's favourite jigs, tapping her foot in time with her fingers' ministrations. *Twitch, flick, tip, tap*: the drift snarls around Rowe's slender limbs, tangles in her dull hair, stretches her bones like saltwater taffy. A third swig and her braids unravel, strands sliming down to her waist before writhing skywards; sage seaweed tossing in magic's strange currents. Another mouthful and her skin glimmers, thins to gauze, then hardens into black hide. One last swallow and the empty cup falls, Rowe's scarred hands now gripless, pelican blades shrunk into swamp-green hoofs—but *it's enough*, Winni knows, this time she's done enough—and the mer-mustang's hind legs are lengthening, rearing, her tough flanks a-shimmer with salmonid scales, tentacle-tail sprouting from a powerful rump.

'Damn you, Rowe! Open up!'

The fey beast snickers at the b'y's miserable yodelling. Her fetlock-fins slap the worn timber floor, part canter, part dance. Liquid garnet eyes shine in her fearsome, elegant face. Her velvet muzzle grins, revealing a pale row of scrimshaw teeth.

'Just look at you,' Winni says and when the kelpie whickers, shaking her beautiful, oil-slick head, its sleek belly rumbles with Rowe's laughter.

'Ha! We're in, lads!' With a screech, the doorframe shrieks and

Rankin Orr bulls in through a flurry of splinters. Coveralls soaked and sandpapered with grit, ginger hair slicked above a pickled-beet face, he's a fatter, fresher version of the bald ox ploughing in behind him. The pair of them scuffle, all bearings lost, while Marl goes on a-hammering at the trapdoor's underside—but Winni's not afraid. These lads aren't but bluff and bluster, they're punctured blowfish, they're *naught* now that Rowe's been reborn.

A creature of hope and horror.

A night-mare roaring, rampant, *rampaging*.

Brutal hoofs strike a series of raw-steak *thwacks*, a gallop of welts and fractures. Her kin scuttle backwards, skidding out the door like ice blocks off a fishmarket stall, a chaotic, slippery mess. They trip on the threshold, crack elbows on the hut's landing, skin smacking the boards as they crab-scramble away from the kelpie's relentless pummelling.

Rowe *could* chase them, pulp them, mash them to mince, stamp them into stains—but what's the point? They're puny beneath her. They're stupid.

They're ants.

She snorts a great gust of disdain—then *bolts*.

Avoiding the stairs, the strand, the cove and the lake-riddled marshes beyond, Rowe turns sharp out the door, sprints alongside Winni's hut, then hurtles down the jetty. Flailing to their feet, Rowe's kin scurry after her, arms outstretched, stubbornly grasping. Don't bother, Winni thinks as the lads run, as they *reach*. Trying to catch a kelpie's like bailing a boat with a sieve. Harnessing trade winds with a butterfly net. Clipping a girl's wings to keep her from flying.

Rowe is a gulfstream shearing the seaward boards.

She's freedom-fast.

She's already gone.

Smiling, Winni snugs her cloak tight while the mare charges to the pier's end, her feather-steeped spell boosting Rowe as she leaps, as she soars, as she dives.

'Go on after her now, b'ys,' Winni says with a chuckle at the men. 'I dare you.'

Finally off the ladder, Marl climbs the stairs to her house three at a time. Joining his brothers—*too late*—he blunders right past her, chasing the last gust of Rowe's descent. The cool splash of waves welcoming her home.

Three plump terns bob in the late afternoon shallows, nattering like housewives at a garland-gathering. Distracted and full of minnows, they're primed for netting, juicing, stewing. Winnifletch crosses her arms. Burrows her feet deeper into the sand. Leaves the little gossips to float. Her gear is stowed upstairs on shelves and in cupboards, her back and joints aflame from the day's spinning, her insides wrung out like yesterday's laundry. She can't muster the will to bag any more birds. Not now. Maybe not ever.

She desperately needs rest.

The incoming tide soothes her swollen ankles, sucking and spitting out her skirts. If she stands here long enough, Winni thinks, it'll lap the ache from her calves, soak the scream from her hips and maybe, eventually, slick the hitch from her erratic ticker. Shivering, she slides both hands into her cloak's vacant pockets and wonders what else might fit in there. If the treasures she's lost really were the sum of her parts. Her truest stories. Her inheritance and legacy.

Maybe, she thinks, lifting, reburying her feet.

Maybe not.

The air is languid, the tin sky cotton-muffled, the sea a lazy stone-grey. It's almost peaceful, Winni thinks, now the hubbub is settled, the men fled like whipped hounds, and Rowe off in the blue somewhere, supping on pricey mermaids. For hours, she watched the kelpie foam-and-ripple across the swell, dazzled by her fury, her grace. Rowe was breathtaking—*I did it; I did that*—gallop-gliding along sandbars. Prance-plunging into Milligrew's abyss. Breaching the surface like a bold killer whale. Circling back to Winni's shore every so often, Rowe patrolled the inlet while she played, frolicking nearby until she was sure the b'ys were well and truly gone. Until she believed Winni was safe.

The weather's starting to turn ugly, the storm augured in dawn's red sheen slowly churning the furtherest clouds. Winnifletch slushes forward. Skin fish-belly pale, linen layers sodden. She's up to the thighs now, legs senseless, chilled to the core. She's a-thrum with each quivering step. She's rattled. Waves numb her navel, tickle her ribs until she sobs. She shudders herself sober. Steels herself to go on.

The tide creeps in as Winni waits for another flick of horse-fins on the horizon. Or a beat of harpy wings in the heavens. Or a quiet knock at her front door.

She waits.

The water rises.

PREVIOUS PUBLICATION CREDITS

Several of these stories have appeared elsewhere:

- 'Gutted' *Shimmer*, Issue 13, April 2011, 17-21
- 'A Right Pretty Mate', *Dreaming in the Dark*, ed. Jack Dann (PS Publishing, 2016), 91-110
- 'Another Mouth', *The Dark*, Issue 1, 2013 (online)
- 'Out on the Shillingate Isles', *Bitter Distillations*, ed. Mark Beech (Egaeus Press, 2020), 137-164
- 'A Tanglesmithed Tale', *Songs of the Northern Seas*, ed. Mark Beech (Egaeus Press, 2021), 53-64
- 'A Shot of Salt Water', *The Dark*, Issue 8, 2015 (online)
- 'Deep in the Drift, Spinning,' *Beneath Ceaseless Skies*, Issue 312, 2020 (online)

ABOUT THE AUTHOR

Lisa L. Hannett is a Canadian-Australian writer and Associate Professor in Creative Writing at Flinders University. Lisa has had over 80 short stories published in venues including *Clarkesworld*, *Fantasy*, *Weird Tales*, *Apex*, *The Dark* and *Year's Best* anthologies in Australia, Canada and the US. She has won four Aurealis Awards, an Australian National Science Fiction Award, an Australian Shadows Award, and has twice been nominated for a World Fantasy Award. You can find her online at lisahannett.com and on Instagram @LisaLHannett.

instagram.com/LisaLHannett

THANK YOU FOR BUYING THIS
BRAIN JAR PRESS COLLECTION

To receive special offers, bonus content, and info on
new releases and other great reads, visit us
online at www.BrainJarPress.com/newsletter